CHRISTMAS MIRACLES
Hope for the Holidays

Compiled by
AT ABOVE and BEYOND

www.ataboveandbeyond.com

Copyright © 2023 At Above And Beyond. All rights reserved. No part of this publication may be reproduced, distributed or transmuted in any form or by any means, including photocopying, recording or other electronic and mechanical methods, without the publisher's prior written permission.

Compiled and Published by At Above And Beyond
E: ataboveandbeyond@gmail.com
W: ataboveandbeyond.com

This book is for entertainment purposes only. Nothing in this book or any affiliations with this book is a substitute for legal, medical or psychological help and advice. If you are in need of help, please seek out a professional for support.

ISBN: 9798864494066

"Christmas Miracles: where love shines brightest, hope knows no bounds, and Dreams Take Flight."

INTRODUCTION

What is AAAB Christmas Miracle?

We launched the idea of this book both last Christmas and back at Christmas in July this past summer. It became a growing Christmas Miracle of its own!

We wanted to do something to give back to our community and the world but had no idea how to bring that to fruition. The idea of this book was birthed from our desire to be part of the change we desire in this world. As a new small business without a lot of resources, we relied on Spirit to show us how to proceed and this book is the result of that. We offered this book without contribution fees to our writers which enabled more inclusiveness to authors who might not otherwise be able to write with us.

The making of this book became our miracle and the stories within its pages speak to the possibilities of the miracles in everyday life, not just at Christmas. The potential for a miracle lives within your belief that they are possible.

Through this book, we extend to you the invitation to believe in the possibility of miracles in your life as well. Whatever the miracle you are looking for, we invite you to believe that it is within your reach. Ask for what you desire and believe.

May the stories within the following pages inspire you to have Hope in the possibilities of miracles in your life.

We thank our Authors for their wonderful contributions!

Meet The Authors

ANITA DJURKOVIC

Anita knows what it's like to experience both deep valleys and mountaintop views, but it is the deep valleys that have given her the ability to serve with a level of humility that makes others feel seen, heard, and loved right where they are. Working in tandem with God's grace, Anita owns and operates Ethereal Energy Interfaith Officiants, where she gets to bring her deep roots of spiritual formation, her extensive education, and her compassion through understanding significant loss into people's most cherished ceremonies. Anita has not just overcome many challenges but she has used each one as a brick to build a sturdy foundation from which to serve. It is from here she can show others what is possible for them in their own lives.

ANNE JOANNETTE-WHITE

Anne is a grateful soul, who continues to evolve through life's experiences and lessons. Learning to trust her higher self, she discovers feelings of hope, joy and love during her journeys. She is proud to be contributing to this, her sixth collaborative book with AAAB.

This chapter is dedicated to all who can let their inner child rejoice in the day-to-day small miracles of love in one's "family" (Whatever way you choose to define "family").

BB ELIZABETH CARVER

BB Elizabeth Carver lives in the Niagara Region, Ontario Canada. She is the author of a book called "Resilient Eyes." Her book offers an insight into how she used her imagination to turn her childhood trauma into inspirational success keys. She is an Executive Fitness Coach Practitioner, Registered Fitness Appraiser, Inspirational Motivational Coach and Activity Program Director. Her company is called Kindfulness Therapy. She works with her partner, who is a psychotherapist, specializing in anxiety healing and motivational plans, offering online classes, workshops, in-person and remote therapy. She has over 20 years of experience in personal training and fitness coaching and is a former health club owner and aerobics instructor. Her website is kindfulnesstherapy.ca. You can email her at bb@kindfulnesstherapy.ca

BETTY LONG

Betty is a sensitive caring nurturing soul with the heart of a mother. The oldest of five children, she learned at a young age to be a nurturing leader to her siblings. As a Special Needs Educational Assistant, she continued with that nurturing energy. Married to the same man for 51 and a half years, she has learned a thing or two about commitment along the way. All her adult life, there has always been room at Betty's table for someone needing Love and occasionally, even a few moved in. Now retired and widowed, Betty is embarking on a new journey of discovering what is next for her. Certainly, through her commitment to her Faith, that sensitive, caring and nurturing soul will emerge once again.

BILL HARLE

Bill loves writing poetry. It's a gift from God and he's been writing for a number of years now. He likes to share his work so that others will see what a great God we have. He hopes that people will be encouraged, strengthened, and inspired to seek God with all of their hearts. He's thankful for this opportunity to share his work and his faith with whoever may read it.

BUNNY KEATING

Bunny is the founder of Bunny Keating Soul Coach, which provides Personal and Business Coaching through connecting to her client's soul. This is done through various forms of Spiritual services. She is also the co-founder of At Above And Beyond, with her business partner Maggie Morris-Mingay where they currently have a weekly podcast about Spiritual topics. They assist others in working on their own healing through writing and offering those stories of healing to the world as published authors in At Above And Beyond Collaborative Books. Feel free to reach out by email at bunnykeating@gmail.com and follow her on social media.

CHRISTINA O'REGAN

Christina is a 32-year-old stay-at-home mom and a first-time author with a passion for the written word. Christina started showing interest in reading and writing and at a young age she could always be found with a book in her hand or paper and a pencil. Christina lives in New Brunswick with her partner Patrick and their 5 children. Other than soaking up every moment with her loved ones, Christina enjoys cooking, baking, spending time outside and running a small crafting business creating personalized items.

EMILIE WHITE

Photo Credit Amos Photography

    I am Emilie White, a daughter, a sister, a wine enthusiast and a wedding coordinator. I love and appreciate every moment spent with family and friends while creating new memories with them, especially if it's by the ocean. I am thrilled to be writing my third chapter in a collaborative book, and expressing how blessed I am to have been raised with such amazing Christmas memories and experiences.

    Special thanks to both my parents for taking Sarah and me on these trips for multiple years.

    I never took any of them for granted.

IANTHA&JOHN JINKS

We are John & Iantha Jinks, Mom & Da to two amazing adult children, who with their wonderful spouses have blessed us with three beautiful & brilliant granddaughters. We met when we had both all but given up on love and decided to give love just one more chance. This year marks 15 years since we said "I do!" and officially started our lifelong dance together. We have danced on many beaches in the Caribbean, at the Mayan Ruins, on Parliament Hill in Ottawa, in 10 countries, 3 Provinces, 7 States and even in Dollarama or grocery stores if a special song comes on the radio. So our advice to you is: 'Find your hot button and dance all over it! We are now using our life experiences to help coach others and point them to God!

You can reach John&Iantha at jinksleadership@gmail.com

JODY SWANNELL

Jody Swannell is a local author from Ontario residing in the beautiful Region of Waterloo. Her love of adventure has taken her on incredible trips, like visiting castles in Scotland, shopping in the West Edmonton Mall, snorkelling in Jamaica and photographing glaciers during an Alaskan cruise. She enjoys coffee, wine, and movie popcorn—in that order.

Her goal is to keep readers eagerly turning pages while trying to guess what happens next—occasionally adding a splash of romance here and there to spice things up a bit. She loves writing contemporary fiction in the mystery, thriller, and sci-fi genres.

KIM CUBITT

Kim Cubitt was born in Sault St. Marie, Ontario, but has spent most of her life living in New Dundee, Ontario.

She has a distinct love for all things macabre, monster, supernatural, and mystery. Halloween is by far her favourite time of the year.

She can normally be found with her dog on her lap, reading a good book or enjoying a spooky movie or TV show when she isn't writing all about all the voices in her head.

LEONA JOANNETTE

    A sincere Soul with a big heart of Love, who was destined to be a Teacher from a very young age, Leona has always been either mothering or teaching for all of her adult life. When retirement came, the teaching and the loving just changed from children in school to everyone she met along the path of life. Leona has learned, in her golden years, to authentically love and appreciate who she is and all the wisdom and knowledge that comes with it. She now puts pen to paper to share her wisdom with the world.

LINDA RODGERS

    Linda is a kind and caring soul who wishes to honour her journey by offering her authentic self to the world. She chooses to share her healing journey publicly to lend her support to those who are doing so privately. Linda understands the human suffering that can follow a traumatic experience; and in the wake of a worldwide crisis that gave rise to increased stress, adversity, and hardships, there has never been a better time to talk about post-traumatic stress. As a mental health advocate, author, and presenter, Linda expands on her personal and professional experiences to educate, to hold space for open dialogue, and promote healing in the hope survivors will seek early diagnosis, treatment, and support.
Reach out to Linda at Linda.rodgers.author@gmail.com

MAGGIE MORRIS-MINGAY

Maggie is an Authentic Caring, Sensitive Soul with a Passion for nurturing others with her Soul Love. Maggie lives her gifts of service to humanity through her generosity and her ability to ignite the flame in others to see their limitless possibilities. Maggie uses her intuition and connection with Spirit to be an example of strength and courage to all she meets. Now as an Author, Public Speaker, Life Coach, Mindfulness Master/Mentor, Meditation Facilitator, Government of Ontario Certified Officiant and Death Doula, Maggie continues to pursue her passions as well as help those she connects with to find Healing.

You can reach Maggie through her website at www.whispersofwisdom.ca or through Facebook

MELANIE BEAMER

Mélanie extends her gifts of service to humanity as a published Author, Public Speaker, Medium, and Oracle card reader and Channels weekly messages from Mother Earth Gaïa. She is also an Energetic Healer, Life Coach and Mentor. Mélanie is a Public Speaker and has given presentations with World Unity Week Events, oneworld.earth for the 99 Days of Peace Through Unity and Peace Week. Mélanie's mission is to serve humanity individually, collectively and unified through her kindness and unconditional love, talents and divine gifts.

You can contact Mélanie via
Email: yourinnerinfinityconnection@outlook.com
Website: melaniebeamer.ca

ROSE BOURASSA

Rose Bourassa had a distinguished career as a procurement specialist.

Away from work, she has worn many hats: mother, grandmother, student, and teacher. Recently retired, she has become an international bestselling author and serves her community by volunteering with her local library and, most recently, the local Relay for Life Team. She holds board offices with both groups.

She strives to learn something new every day to keep her mind sharp and interact with her grandkids to keep her young at heart. She is currently preparing for a second career as an evidential medium.

You can contact Rose via email at Remnick@aol.com

SARAH WHITE

    Hello everyone, my name is Sarah White, and I am thrilled to include a chapter in my second book compiled by At Above And Beyond. I am someone who prioritizes spending time with family, friends and my partner, Patrick. I am beyond happy to have all of them in my life as they are my biggest supporters in everything I do. If I am not spending time with them, you can find me working alongside some of the most intelligent and love-worthy kids that I have the privilege to call my students or cuddled up on the couch watching a classic Disney movie.

    Thank you and Merry Christmas to all!

SHERRY HARLE

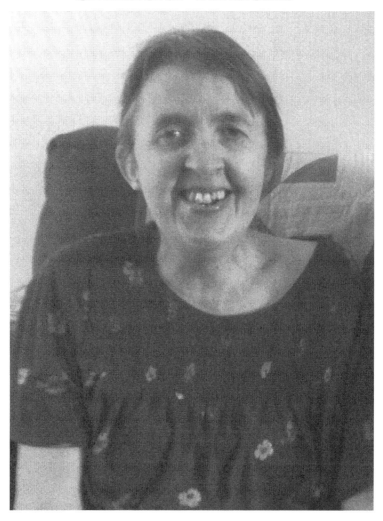

Sherry is a kind, thoughtful lady who loves people, purple, puns and poetry. Born in Cape Breton, N.S., Sherry appreciated and enjoyed experiencing the beauty of her surroundings. It helped spark her imagination and provided great inspiration. Sherry enjoys writing about God and she hopes that her works will draw people to Him and His great love.

SUSAN DIANE

    I believe that most people make their greatest contribution and largest impact one person at a time, yet through my writing I hope to have a positive influence in a wider circle. In contrast to my working career as a graduate engineer and a chartered professional accountant, I am currently honouring a lifelong passion for literature. In my first novel three voices spanning successive generations, recount a tale of extraordinary, because aren't we all in our own unique way, twentieth-century women? Consistent with my inclination to support individuals with personal money management, I provide life coaching, with an emphasis on wealth health and financial fitness.

    You may contact me at thestoryteller@susandiane.ca

TAMMY BRAZEAU

Tammy is a loving devoted wife, stepmother and grandmother. Her life is full of the love and support of her family.

This is her third time as a published author in a collaborative book with At Above And Beyond.

Writing has been a healing journey. It's her self-expression.

Author Submissions

UNCONDITIONAL CHRISTMAS!
By Anita Djurkovic

I never understood the whole Christmas was a time of joy, love, and hope concept. My Christmas experiences, while growing up, were ones marred with adult freakouts and demands, a lot of screaming and worse.

Now, in stating this, I do not want you to think that my life was without privilege. I received more than my fair share of fantastic Christmas gifts. I had every Barbie, game and book that a young kid could ever want. Those gifts were not without their conditions. They became a form of currency, an exchange for my self-esteem. I guess that is why as a grown-up sometimes gifts did not mean that much to me. In the past, those who loved me, I am sure felt shortchanged sometimes by my lack of enthusiasm at receiving gifts.

When things have conditions, it is hard to simply trust. I am better at this now though.

As I got older, the weight of my youth and subsequent struggles sometimes left my spirit irreparably broken, so I sought to remedy my brokenness by popping pills, getting blackout drunk and using other incredibly unhealthy coping mechanisms which endangered me in countless ways.

Living in the past stopped me from living, and led me to not trusting anyone, I found myself trapped in a never-ending shame cycle. I numbed myself to escape. During this time, I would become horribly depressed over the Christmas season and into January and February, which once landed me on a 21-day hold in a psychiatric facility.

The guilt and shame that I carried were dangerously becoming my entire personality. I would ask for God's forgiveness every single time that I had overindulged or hurt myself or done something to put myself in danger, which was very commonplace.

Deep intuition and this ability to hear God since childhood aided me in envisioning a better life because I knew there was more for me. I knew God was listening to all my begging and empty promises, that had now become true prayers. So, by the grace of that same loving God, I found the faith and strength to turn my life around, just like that. I remember the exact date, May 23rd.

It is a strange thing when you decide to return your life to God and drop your act. The years to follow, in my case anyway, were some of the most difficult years of my life. So many hills and valleys, you know.

Then after about 10 years, drug-free, I had a car accident that left me not only with painful physical complications but also completely launched my CPTSD into the stratosphere. This was a time in my life which proved exceedingly difficult. Months and months of doctors' appointments did not bring me the answers that I was so desperately seeking. However, due to my refusal to take medication, the very people who were supposed to support me and understand or care were now the ones placing conditions. This conditional exchange was far too familiar, so I decided to dig in my heels and do things differently, proactively and with the knowledge of so many lessons learned instead of becoming a victim.

The battles I was enduring became manageable because the ones I had already conquered seemed to lead the way. I would no longer be dismissed by the specialists that I continuously objected to their wanting to put me back on strong medications. I already knew what control they could have over my life and what it could lead to. I would never go back to that way of living knowing the grip it would have on me, I would not be able to survive it.

I knew deep in my soul that I would rather feel joy, pain, and agony than feel nothing, the way I used to.

There was an actual Guardian Angel on my side. They were a compassionate and caring person who knew my past, and my struggles, and more so, this Guardian Angel would always be the first one to high-five me every year that I celebrated being drug-free. This Guardian Angel was there, as always, to offer me encouragement and support, going as far as to write a letter on my behalf, saying how far I had come and the importance for me to receive holistic support and natural treatment options.

Tragically, in mid-December, not long after his generous letter of support was written, he passed away. His death was a huge heartbreak for me, my family and all who knew him. His presence continues to live in my heart, these many years later.

In the aftermath of the sad news of his passing, it seemed like it would be another gloomy Christmas, but then, a short while later, I realized that this Guardian Angel was the catalyst to me receiving the holistic support that I needed going forward. I felt a renewed sense of purpose, on cloud nine and was so glad that I listened and heard God's voice saying, "Don your armour and keep fighting," as he had said many times before.

Now, after all these years, this is only one of the many stories that I hope to share with others who are still trapped in their own dark places. I am armoured with resilience. I can love people with a greater vulnerability, unconditionally and promise to never use my love or my gifts as a form of collateral. My love comes without conditions.

I am grateful for what has resulted after every struggle, and hardship that has peppered my past. It is not the trauma that makes you stronger, it is the fighting spirit and faith that does. I am grateful now for every Christmas and I have been for about a decade. My prayer is that this small Christmas miracle can remind you, as it does me, about the power of faith, love, hope and resilience, and reminds us to never give up, even in the face of huge adversity. A reminder that miracles are individual and miracles are real!

FROM HEAVEN TO US
By Leona Joannette

WOW! Unbelievable! This is the most memorable time of the year to reminisce…HIS birthday! He was born as a Miracle to Mary with the assistance of the HOLY SPIRIT. Joseph, his earth father, was present at His side… This, the BELIEVERS celebrate on the 25th day of December, depending on the religion in which they participate. Jesus was offered to us as a free GIFT…A MIRACLE! At HIS Last Supper, Jesus offered his LIFE… GOD'S GIFT of self…A MIRACLE!

Another example of a Miracle is our birth. We have no idea where we came from nor where we will end up after this life. But in between both periods, for a short lapse of time that is allowed to us, why not truly profit from the "adventure" called life?

In a previous collective book, I talked about how we are GIFTS from God. Today, let's try… we are MIRACLES created by GOD. If you let spirituality play an important role in your life, WISDOM led by the SOUL, you will find clarity and peace within… even when facing an oncoming storm. Choose your life path with joy and gratitude in your heart!

We are all "connected." We are all "United." We all belong to one "Universal" light and family. We are precious gifts given by our Father. What a wonderful gift we are! It is a private, personal relationship between the one who gives and the one who receives. The fact with whom one has warm regards or affection demonstrates a BOND BETWEEN SOULS. Yes, this also has been developed in a previous book!

Well, it takes a "Big Bang" in one's life to actually appreciate this relationship... A Miracle! I've learned to love myself first and then appreciate where I am in life. I used to walk seven or eight floors of my apartment building using stairs in between floors, but not anymore. I've learned that the best time to make friends is before you need them... And this also involves family...

The week before August 5, 2023, I received signs of what was coming... pain around my heart area which I ignored. The night before the fifth around 10 PM, I felt a bolt of lightning hitting my forehead above my eyes... That certainly scared me! My right hand went flying over my eyes. As I kept my eyes closed, I heard, "Breathe... Breathe..." I did what I was "told" to do and eventually calmed down and went to bed. The next morning, everything was back to normal. I did my usual routine.

Later that morning, I noticed that my right hand did not move as usual. I slowly picked up my phone, only to have it fall three times before realizing something was really wrong... I walked slowly, sat down, raised my arms, OK... Smile, OK... Talk... No way! I called my sons who did not answer their phones so I decided to leave a message... To my surprise, only "jargon" would come out... I decided to leave a text... What fun... Especially when my fingers didn't do what I wanted them to do.

After realizing my sons were at the cottage without any reception, I decided to call 911... Of course, I had a problem verbally expressing the information to the dispatcher because I couldn't easily or clearly pronounce anything. I decided to spell my address, my phone number and my name. The dizziness was horrible. It didn't take long, the ambulance was here.... I managed, with determination, to unlock my door to let the paramedics come in. To my surprise, as soon as they started asking a battery of questions, I answered without any hesitation! Go figure..! A MIRACLE? The only problem they found was that I had very high blood pressure...I made a decision to go back to the hospital with them to get a thorough check-up. After many tests, I was diagnosed with having had a "transient stroke" (mini-stroke). I called a taxi later the same day so I could go rest at home. I was given new meds and a referral to the stroke clinic. Feeling weak and tired, I also felt relieved after hearing my sons' voice saying they were on their way back to see me.

Almost 2 weeks passed by and it was time for more tests. The first one was an echo test. Then it was off to the stroke clinic for a series of five more tests. The first of them was a neurological examination. Skilled observations of my ability to answer questions and perform simple tasks were evaluated. That one was easy enough. Next... I believe, was an ECG, an electrocardiogram. An abnormal heart rhythm that may cause blood clots to form was diagnosed. The attendant left the room to review the results of the test.

Within a few seconds, the specialist returned to the room where my son and I were waiting. Placing a chair squarely in front of me and sitting on it, he said that nothing more was being done for me at the clinic today. I was to leave immediately for the emergency department. The attending nurse sat me in a wheelchair and accompanied me all through my exam process. The specialist had called in my arrival and a team of professionals were ready to do their part. They seemed like a flock of birds circling over me with machines, needles, questions, IV, blood tests, blood pressure, heart rhythm... Too high! Too fast! Feeling like a pin cushion wasn't pleasant but they were moving fast and they knew their jobs! They tried to slow down my heartbeat, lower my blood pressure and thin out my blood to prevent another stroke. New meds were administered and the heart rate had to be constantly monitored in case my blood pressure dropped too low.

All this time I was sitting up on a stretcher, and my son was on the other side of the doors, impatiently waiting for the nurse to come and bring him back in. During this time, an announcement was called for a patient crashing! I could only imagine my son's reaction to this... The patient was brought next to me and the crew moved over to her side. After this alert, Claude said his heart was pounding. He wanted to know what was going on. Was it his mom who was crashing? Finally, the nurse brought him in and to his relief, our eyes met and he realized I wasn't the one who "crashed"! This was originally a workday for him, but after what just happened, he gladly stayed by my side for the rest of the day. I truly appreciated his support and presence, while his siblings were patiently waiting for his call.

My test results indicated that my blood pressure and heart rate did come down, but not enough! Pill for this, pill for that... I finally went home being diagnosed with "Atrial Fibrillation" (an irregular heartbeat that can lead to blood clots, and or a stroke). Over a month of tests! Tests! Tests! With no energy, I was left with weakness and dizziness. I move slowly and use a cane when leaving my apartment. During the afternoons, time for rest is usually needed.

From time to time, I still experience a heaviness on the right side of my head and above my eyes... I am comforted with this thought... What if? Could this be My Miracle? What a profound realization! Circumstances could have been so much worse. I could have lost my life! For the initial episode, on that memorable day, I was alone in my apartment.

Alone? No! From the beginning, my Angels were there; my guides took over along with my spiritual allies, and most of all our Creator! I certainly was NOT alone, because all through this ordeal from the first day, I felt so calm, no panic. From realizing something was not right, to calling 911 for help, to speaking to the dispatcher, to the paramedics arriving and helping me, to the ambulance ride to the hospital, to all the tests taken, to finally coming back home that same day… I DID IT! I AM SO PROUD OF MYSELF!

Now that my family and friends know about my situation, I get to witness how the Holy Spirit guides them to show me day-to-day miracles of their help and sincere concern for me. He reminds me to live in Faith, not fear! With positive thinking, every day, I am getting better and stronger. I am truly grateful for God's gifts of love manifested through the presence of family members, friends and all the professionals who took care of me.

Miracles can happen to all of us when we BELIEVE! The simple act of saying. "hello," is a way of saying, "I care," and the beginning of an awe-inspiring ripple effect!

If you could accomplish a miracle in your life, what would it be? Take time to meditate on these different miracle possibilities.

- A great miracle is one of FORGIVENESS! What a powerful feeling once the problem has been solved! Don't wait for other people to excuse themselves. It takes place when we let go of fear and choose to love instead. A miraculous procedure that breaks down the barriers that close our hearts and souls from the most Divine. Choose forgiveness today and experience the love in your life on your spiritual journey.
- The second miracle is one of NATURE! It is where you go outside and connect with nature and fresh air. As you walk in nature, you open yourself up to Divine guidance from heaven and Earth. You can feel the essence of life, love and beauty.
- My favourite miracle is one of PRAYER! All prayers sent to heaven have been heard and answered. We need to be patient on how we receive the answers. Accept them! Fill your prayers with loving thoughts and gratitude!
- WE ARE MIRACLES! Whatever happens in our lives, find the positives! When I see my children, their children, their

children's children… I see them as true miracles! They are the dots that connect the lines from generation to generation. From the past to the present, and to the future! How powerful are we, the "Miracles?" I believe we are made in resemblance to Jesus…our given Miracle! In a Bible story, someone asked: "Jesus, who are you?" Jesus answered: "I AM!" For those who have read my previous chapters… I stress the importance of acknowledging the awareness of one's TRUST and BELIEF in your own, Inner-Outer Beauty and Strength by revealing to yourself, "I AM!"

- Be kind to yourself, and fully accept your present mental, emotional and physical conditions. The result is vital to your happiness. Since energy is the basis of everything, the body is designed to heal itself. As I wake up in the morning, I'd like to remind myself: "My soul is beautiful, my mind is powerful, my heart is made of golden love and I have a lot to be grateful for!" One physical characteristic of mine is a " rounded and curved" upper back. I used to notice other beautiful seniors who walked with curved backs but never considered that I was one of them. I discovered this when my oldest brother entered an Extendicare Home. Wow! What a revelation! I hated my physical stature at the time. But when I saw, close-up, his demeanour, I saw his " wings" spreading out. I would cover his back with my hands and thought: "A wonder…a Miracle." When he passed away to be with our Saviour, I started "seeing" my own "Angel Wings" coming out! A MIRACLE! I proudly walk showing my growing "wings." I appreciate it when my children pass their big hands over them, it feels reassuring. There is love there… Anything you accept fully will lead you into peace. This is the miracle of SURRENDER!

Life has many troubles, but it also has many blessings. Look for them when in doubt, and embrace them. We don't have to be superheroes to be part of God's family! We need to Believe and follow the path He has set for us with positivity and acceptance! I accept the circumstances, facing my own personal healing journey. I am living in the Present!

With the new day comes new strength and new thoughts. Learn from yesterday! Hope for tomorrow!

LEARN FROM THE PAST!

LIVE IN THE PRESENT!

HOPE FOR THE FUTURE!

WHERE'S YOUR MIRACLE?
By Bunny Keating

As I contemplated what to write in this chapter, dedicated to the magic of Christmas Miracles, I was initially uncertain about my own experiences. Had I ever truly encountered a "Christmas Miracle?" While I've certainly enjoyed wonderful Christmases, filled with cherished moments of giving and receiving, I couldn't pinpoint a single miraculous instance. In fact, I had contemplated crafting a fictional narrative for this very submission and even publicly announced this, but here I am now, sharing my genuine voice on this wondrous topic, and I'm elated to add my story to this wonderful book.

My birthday falls on December 18th, and I've always believed that I arrived early into this world to ensure I could partake in an "extra" Christmas, my original due date being in January. My adoration for this holiday runs deep, and it encompasses the entire experience. Picture me as the person who visits the busy mall during the holiday season, captivated by the sight of people bustling about, searching for the perfect gifts for their loved ones. The excitement emanating from them as they carry bags filled with joyous surprises never fails to inspire me. The melodious sounds of Christmas music fill the air, while the scents of cinnamon, cloves, nutmeg, peppermint, and evergreen waft around, weaving a tapestry of seasonal enchantment. The world sparkles with festive decorations, turning every corner into a realm of wonder. I anticipate this time of year with fervour, counting down the days until its arrival.

During my childhood, money was often scarce, but my birthday's proximity to Christmas meant I could use my birthday funds to purchase gifts for others. I took immense joy in gifting heartfelt presents to my loved ones, finding greater satisfaction in giving than receiving. This sentiment still rings true for me today.

One cherished Christmas tradition I hold dear is watching "A Christmas Carol" by Charles Dickens, the 1951 version featuring Alastair Sim as "Scrooge," with my father on Christmas Eve. I can't quite recall how old I was when I first watched it, but the memory is vivid in my mind. I continue this tradition every year, now in memory of my father, who passed away in November 2012. When my children were young, I would set up the movie, sip on eggnog, wrap their presents, and place them beneath the twinkling tree. The tale of discovering the goodness within someone, a power I've come to embrace in my own life, and witnessing their redemption always resonated with me. No matter how grim someone's exterior may appear, there's always a kind soul striving to do their best. It's a message of hope, one that I cherish and continually embrace. This tradition serves as an annual reminder to release any perceived shortcomings from the past year and extend forgiveness to myself—a crucial life lesson in learning to be gentle with oneself.

Now, let's dive into the delectable realm of holiday feasts. Oh, the food! As a first-generation Canadian with Italian, Serbian, and Scottish roots, our family Christmas gatherings were a gastronomic extravaganza. Each family member contributed their specialty dishes, such as Grandma Jean's trifle and my mother's homemade cranberry sauce, turkey with stuffing, mashed potatoes, cheese and cracker platters, Christmas cookies, pea salad, bean bread, and so much more. Our commitment was to ensure that every guest, regardless of dietary restrictions, revelled in their chosen dishes. I recall as a child, eagerly cracking open nuts in their shells, my favourites being Brazil nuts and almonds. This beloved tradition continues as we welcome new members into our family, ensuring their favourites grace our festive table as well.

But perhaps, the most cherished moments revolve around watching my own children experience the enchantment of Christmas mornings—gifts from Santa and stockings brimming with surprises. One Christmas, my youngest, Denton, who was just three years old, made an unconventional request of Santa—a Chia Pet. I scrambled to find one at my part-time job at Walmart, and luckily, we had a special Christmas Gifts section that had Chia Pets. Another year, he yearned for a Fire Truck, and my quest to find one ended on December 22nd, sans packaging, which was nothing short of a holiday miracle. To top it off, we were shopping together as a family, adding an extra layer of excitement. And I'll never forget the year when my eldest son, Topher, at the tender age of seven, stumbled upon the "Santa" wrapping paper hidden in a corner beside the laundry room sink. Thankfully I was able to explain it away, stating that Santa would ask the parents to provide the wrapping paper, and he would magically wrap the presents when he came to deliver them. I just wanted the magic of Santa to last a little bit longer.

There was also a Christmas when uncertainty loomed as to how I would provide gifts for my children. A year earlier, their father and I had separated, leaving me working part-time at Walmart with limited resources for anything beyond the essentials. Then, a remarkable turn of events transpired. The principal of their elementary school, Simcoe Street Public School, contacted me, summoning me to his office without divulging the purpose of our meeting. Anxious, I wondered if it would involve disappointing news about one of my children's academic performance. Little did I know, I was in for an astonishing revelation. Mr. Scott looked at me and said, "I have $1000 for you and your children. An anonymous donor generously contributed this money and requested that I pass it on to a deserving family. We chose you." Shock and joy surged through me in equal measure. To this day, I remain grateful to the incredible stranger whose selfless generosity allowed me to provide my children with a Christmas filled with wonder and delight that year.

The Christmas of 2020 ushered in monumental changes for my family. We moved into a new home on September 27th, marking the end of our 22-year residence in our previous house—the only home my children had ever known since they were 20 and 17. We also welcomed a new member into our household, Sydney, Topher's girlfriend, whom I fondly refer to as the "daughter of my heart." In our new home, we embarked on creating fresh traditions, including acquiring a new Christmas tree. We strategically placed the tree by the front door, allowing passersby to catch a glimpse of its radiant beauty through the window. I vividly recall the day when Sydney and Topher adorned the tree for me. I sat on the couch, attaching hooks to ornaments, some of which were older than the two souls decorating the tree. As they carefully placed each ornament, a sense of pure joy filled the room. The most heartwarming moment was when I told Sydney that she could hang the ornaments anywhere on the tree as she pleased. It was a liberating experience for her, one she had never encountered before. This made my heart sing! This tradition, shared with my children, is one I intend to cherish forever.

You see, the true Christmas Miracles for me are woven into the fabric of every Christmas. There need not be a grand spectacle or extraordinary event. The miracle resides in the joy that envelops me each time I reflect on the Christmas season—an enduring source of wonder that never fails to warm my heart.

May your holiday seasons be filled with unconditional love and happy memories!

LOVE AND FAMILY
By Anne Joannette-White

My most treasured childhood memories are during Christmas time.

As a child, it was traditional to open our gifts at the crack of dawn, go to church with our parents and sing well-known and loved songs and hymns for the celebration of Jesus's birthday. After church, we ALL gathered at my grandparents' house for the Christmas feast. Family gatherings in their home were always captivating and full of excitement. The men were in the living room, the women in the kitchen and us children, we were all in the basement gathered around the Christmas tree. There was so much going on in every room! Laughing, singing, teasing, cooking, drinking and a whole lot of love! Every year my mémére would knit socks, hats, scarfs, mittens and slippers to make sure that every single grandchild had a gift under the Christmas tree handmade, with love, by her. My pépére would pass around candy canes to us with a sparkle in his eyes. My grandparents were so happy and proud to be surrounded by their 10 children, spouses and many grandchildren!

I remember my pépére dressing up as Santa Claus and walking up our street. To my surprise, Santa Claus was coming into my house! I was so excited! How special is that? My squeals of joy woke up my brothers and there he was, Santa, in our house! WOW! Other years, when all the cousins were gathered at my grandparents' house, Santa would show up there and bring gifts for all of us. We were the luckiest kids indeed! For New Year's Day, my pépére was proud to give his family the yearly blessing. The miracle of pure love of family, through my eyes and experience as a child, will always stay magical for me.

The years passed by and I found myself going through adolescence. Commercialism became more important and I started to understand this part of Christmas. It seemed exciting. My need to buy gifts to please others was obvious. My dad, in my teenage mind, turned into Scrooge during the weeks before Christmas. He disliked Christmas time very much. Every year he would tell us: "You are spoiled and you don't understand how hard I had it." He finally shared with us his sad reminders of his childhood Christmases.

As a child, his dad left them alone on the farm while he went off to work during the Christmas holiday in a logging camp. All my mémére could give her children in their Christmas stockings were peanuts, an apple and sometimes, an orange. My dad also hated crowds and shopping (I learned later that he always feared that we wouldn't like his gifts). My mom was stressed with so many details to take care of, she was the commander! She was equipped with her "to-do" list and told all of us what needed to be done. A well-decorated house was very important for her. She was exceptionally particular about the tinsel on the tree… I remember one year, I just gave up perfectly placing hundreds of tinsel strands like my mom did and just threw them all over…well, you guessed it… Mom wasn't amused… (At least she never asked me to do that job again!)

We hosted dinners, went out to dinners and had a lot of shopping and preparation to do. My mother was often responsible for the children's mass at church and with all the last minute details on her mind I watched as she flawlessly guided the children to celebrate the joy of Christ. The miracle, during my teenage years, was that I realized the emotional and financial pressure my parents endured to make each Christmas completely magical and memorable for us.

My perspective and understanding of the importance of the "work" that is involved with preparing the magic which brings and shares joy and love with family and friends through the Christmas season began to evolve and my perspective of what was important shifted.

Many years later as young parents, my husband and I decided that we wanted to create our own family Christmas tradition. We wanted to give our two daughters a trip to the Caribbean during the Christmas holidays. Every Year we would either spend Christmas or New Year's on a beach. Our first trip was, obviously to me, the most memorable one. It was the first plane ride for the girls, the first Christmas away from slush and snow, the first Christmas on a beach and the first Christmas to see Christmas lights on the palm trees. The girls did realize the difference in culture and in tradition in the Caribbean. Let's just say they were surprised at how thin Santa Claus was, and how strange it was to see him, arriving on the Sea-Doo instead of arriving with his reindeer.

On that first Christmas morning away from home, the girls and I went to visit the manger. We saw beautiful statues representing the first Christmas. I appreciated having the opportunity to celebrate the birth of Christ with my girls. We sang "Happy Birthday" to Jesus and I followed with an explanation of the symbolism of the shepherds and wise men. "We give and receive gifts at Christmas because the shepherds and the wise men brought their own gifts to Jesus." As the girls got older, they never forgot the importance of giving to others, especially during this time of year. Back home, we often participated in food and toy drives at our school and church. On later trips to the Caribbean, my daughters decided to bring some of their own toys and clothing with them to be able to share and give to local families. The girls will never forget the miracle of bringing love and joy to others….

Last year, thanks to a major snowstorm, I was faced with spending Christmas missing some of my precious family. A travel ban was put out, highways were closed and my daughter and her boyfriend who live 30 minutes away were stuck in their freezing apartment. Christmas morning, my husband did go out to "test" the roads and surprised me with my own miracle. He had the kids in the car with him… I received the most precious gift that day…my family under one warm roof. I didn't need commercial gifts. I had the gift of LOVE and the love of being together.

Throughout my life, I have been truly blessed to have been surrounded by family during Christmas. I hold dear the first family of Christmas, Mary, Joseph, and Jesus. I hold close to my heart my cherished childhood memories at Christmas time, and I do find myself pausing every year, closing my eyes and taking myself back to that small yellow house in my hometown where the miracles of Love and Family were abundant. When I started my own family, I was disappointed at not being able to give my children the exact childhood experience I had with a big family but, by creating new family traditions and memories, my daughters have their own versions of Christmas miracle stories that they will one day share with their own children.

Wishing you and your family a Merry Christmas every day of the year.

CHILDHOOD CHRISTMAS
By Betty Long

Christmas was a fun time, when we went to bed the bare tree was sitting in the living room. In the morning it was decorated and there were presents from "Santa", I found out years later most of the Santa presents were from my mom's aunt. One year my parents took a picture of my sister playing with a broken clock in front of the tree full of gifts. On Christmas morning we opened our socks, which usually had fruit and some candy, in the hall outside my parents' bedroom. Once my brother received a package in his that was wrapped in foil. The rest of us were complaining that we didn't get that until he opened it to find horse manure inside. He was not impressed with the gift.

One year I was sick and not sleeping when Santa came. My parents told me I better pretend to be asleep when Santa came and not get out of my bed. In a few minutes, there were bells outside and a knock at the door. When Mom opened the door Santa said he was in a hurry because one of the reindeer was injured. He asked if my parents could decorate the tree and put out the presents which they agreed to do. In the morning there were hoof marks and sled marks in the driveway.

Getting the tree was an ordeal, my dad wanted it to be perfect and if it wasn't he would add branches. Sometimes he got angry if he couldn't get it just right. So, one year, my brother and I decided to get a tree. We went to the woods, cut it down and dragged it home. When Dad came home it was standing in the living room. My father said he would have to fix it up but we refused to allow that, telling him this is our tree and he couldn't change it. Whenever anyone dropped in, Dad was quick to tell them that we had gotten the tree.

CHRISTMAS WAKE-UP
By Betty Long

One Christmas Eve, my daughters who had just moved from a shared double bed to bunk beds decided to sleep in the same bunk bed. During the night the pillows got pushed against the night light, it heated and caught fire. One of the girls woke up but seeing the fire froze. Thank God her twin woke up and started screaming, "FIRE!" Our son woke up and opened the bathroom window, took a breath of fresh air then went back to bed. We were able to get outside. All was well, the fire department came and cut a hole in the wall to make sure there wasn't a fire inside the walls. They then put a large fan in the window to suck out the smoke.

Since we were all awake 3 a.m. we opened presents while the smoke cleared out of the upstairs. After everyone calmed down we went back to bed and later in the morning, someone phoned, and they were surprised that we were still asleep until we shared our miracle story.

LOOKING FOR THE CHRISTMAS MIRACLES

By Maggie Morris-Mingay

I used to dislike Christmas for all it "wasn't." What a way to start a story about Christmas Miracles! Yet it was my truth.

I believe that very often we can easily get caught up in the "Hallmark" version of what Christmas should be that we lose sight of the true meaning and essence of the holiday.

Christmas is about the giving, not the getting, although the two are often woven together in such a magical way that they can become one…….Maggie

---

As a child, I remember Christmas as a time of arguing, yelling, disagreements, and disappointment with a little sprinkling of joy mixed in from time to time.

Our family, to say the least, was less than rich and our tree was never overflowing with gifts like the children of today.

Our Christmas Stockings were made up of fruit, nuts, some candies and a couple chocolates if we were lucky. The gifts would usually consist of socks, and underwear, along with pajamas or knitted slippers from my grandma and, if Santa came to our house, there would be the toy of our dreams.

For as far back as I can remember, decorating the tree was the worst evening ever. Although it always began with the excitement of hot chocolate and a box of chocolates, it most often ended with my father yelling that the tree was either not standing correctly, or the decorations were not as they should've been.

That was my childhood memory of Christmas and all it "wasn't."

I can happily say that it has improved since then.

One Christmas Miracle came into my life early in January 1987, with that previous Christmas spent in the Nova Scotia Maternity Hospital in a darkened room. There was no tree that I recall, no celebrations or mistletoe just one sick momma-to-be, praying that her baby would grow safely inside her very sick body. Although I didn't feel sick, I remember the nurses telling me that I was one of the sickest women in that maternity ward of the hospital. That year my Christmas Miracle was that my little baby girl stayed safe and sound inside her mommy-to-be, being born absolutely healthy and completely unaffected by the events that had preceded her birth on January 5th. That was our Christmas Miracle!

That little girl grew up to facilitate a few other Christmas Miracle moments.

Christmas is about the giving, not the getting, although the two are often woven together in such a magical way that they can become one.

It was early in the day one Christmas Eve when my daughter came to me frantically announcing that we needed to do something! She had just received a Facebook alert from someone she knew that a young single mom of three in our town had been forgotten in the Christmas Hamper Program. That is a program where people in the community sponsor a needy family for Christmas and buy them gifts.

Somehow this young girl's sponsor had been missed and there would be no gifts coming to her family on Christmas Eve. My daughter in frantically panicked state cried, that we needed to "do something!" Insisting, "Mom, I have some money can't we just go to Walmart and buy them some stuff?" Very soon after we were scurrying around the local Walmart with all the other last-minute shoppers hurrying to provide a last-minute Christmas to this family. We quickly bought toys for the three children and something for mom, a Turkey with all the trimmings, some groceries, Christmas candies and even some wrapping paper. We managed to drop them off to this young mom before the sun went down.

I guess the response to that plea for help on Facebook that day was larger than anyone could have ever imagined as my daughter showed me a post later that evening from the young mom thanking everyone for the Christmas Miracle and asking people to stop delivering gifts to her house as she had more stuff than they could possibly use.

That Christmas, my daughter showed me that Christmas was in the giving not in the getting yet the two were certainly intertwined.

It was the best Christmas ever that year, our smiles were bigger, not just because of what we gave but because of how Love showed up in our town!

Christmas is about the giving, not the getting, although the two are often woven together in such a magical way that they can become one.

Another Christmas Miracle involving my daughter I have written about before, but the story bears repeating in this book for sure.

My daughter struggled in her early adult years because of an unthinkable childhood trauma she had endured. At one point she had run away from home and after time ended up in a group home facility in another country. It was a devastating few years for the whole family, including her, but that Christmas there was a miracle in the making.

In the months leading up to the holidays, I didn't know how I would ever make it through the Christmas season not knowing the whereabouts of my child. Without understanding the "why" I had kept picking up little things for her when I was shopping, bringing them home and putting them in a shoebox. I had no idea why I was buying these things or how I would give them to her as I had no idea where she was.

All that changed, when out of the blue one day my phone rang and my little girl was on the other end of the line. She proceeded to tell me that she was okay and was calling to let me know that she was safe and now living in a group home in Florida. By the end of that call, I had the address of where my little girl was living so I could send her the box I had been filling for her for Christmas.

On Christmas Day, I received a call from her telling me that she received the box and the Christmas Miracle that went along with it. She proceeded to tell me that, from the day she had arrived at the group home, she had been keeping a little list of things she needed to get if she ever got any money. Everything on her list was in the box that I had sent to her. The Christmas Miracle to this momma was not so much that she got the things on her list, but that God had allowed her momma to be the one fulfilling that need.

Christmas is about the giving, not the getting, although the two are often woven together in such a magical way that they can become one.

So often we are unable to look past the pain of something we may be experiencing to see a miracle in it.

Sometimes our most traumatic painful experiences can hold the most profound miracles when we look past the pain to catch a glimpse of the miracle.

Are you looking for a Christmas Miracle?

Do you believe?

Are you looking?
Can you dare to believe through the eyes of a child in the possibility of a Christmas Miracle?

When we quiet the noise around us, we can sometimes hear the angels singing and feel the warmth of their embrace. If you are looking for your miracle just close your eyes and let your heart speak it to your soul. Let your soul bring it to the heavens on angels' wings.

Often those miracles come wrapped in painful life circumstances, yet they are no less miracles.

Are you like me and looking at what Christmas "wasn't"?

I invite you to see the Christmas Miracle you truly need.

I pray you find your Christmas Miracle this year!

Christmas is about the giving, not the getting, although the two are often woven together in such a magical way that they can become one……Maggie

CHRISTMAS PRESENT
By Christina O'Regan

As a little girl, I remember all of the joyous feelings and thoughts I would have around Christmas time. I would wait patiently for Mom to bake a batch of whipped shortbread cookies - the ones with the red and green frosting and sprinkles that just melt in your mouth while you're daydreaming and wondering, "Will it be a white Christmas this year? Is Santa going to bring me that personal CD player I have been dying to have? Or maybe this year's holiday Barbie?"

I wondered about many things. "Will I go to Nana and Papa's home for the holidays this year?" Christmases spent at Nana and Papa's house were always my favourite. I felt so special when Papa would call me over to sit right next to him on the couch and talk about everything since our last visit. I cherished the smell of homemade bread baking in the air, and I admired Nana's collection of teacups, saucers, and silver spoons. I often imagined having a tea party with them, holding my pinky out to be fancy. Still to this day, thinking about the smells and remembering all the memories made throughout the years brings me right back, making me feel like I'm living in that moment, in the present. I count down the seconds before my last bite of a cookie is completely melted away, just like the days left until Christmas day finally arrives. I hope Mom and Dad like the homemade ornament I made for them at school this year.

I have since grown up and become a mother myself, and when I think of Christmas, I am still wondering, just like that little girl I used to be, while I'm tasting those same melt-in-your-mouth cookies that I am now making for my own children. A smile comes across my face as I allow the last of my whipped shortbread cookie to melt away, thinking about my children waiting for a cookie and watching them get lost in their own daydreams as they take their first bite. Are they thinking about a white Christmas too? Are they wondering if Santa is going to bring them that new game or outfit they haven't stopped talking about, which, of course, is already wrapped and tucked away, waiting for their excitement on Christmas day? I think I might be more excited for them to open their presents than they are. But as a parent, I just live for every moment I get to see their eyes light up and the joy on their faces.

    The true gift of Christmas has never been the presents or the cookies but rather who they are shared with, making lasting memories and creating traditions that may be passed down through the generations. This year on Christmas morning, while I'm sitting back sipping my coffee beside my partner on the couch, we will watch our children happily dig out their gifts from under the Christmas tree, sorting the labels to find which ones belong to them. I will be imprinting these memories into my mind for safekeeping, wondering when they grow up and become adults, will they also daydream about their own children? Will they make the same Christmas cookies and listen to the same Christmas music as I do them as my parents did for me?

    Excited little squeals bring my attention back, and I want to stay in this moment as long as I can. Five faces smiling, ready to open present number one, the fireplace on making us feel all fuzzy and warm, with Christmas music playing quietly in the background. Soon, the aroma of turkey dinner with all the fixings and freshly baked bread rolls will start to fill our home. These memories will last longer than anything else I could ever give them. Being present will always be the best present I can give my children and will be the present they cherish

CHRISTMAS GIFTS
By BB Elizabeth Carver

One of the most beloved Christmas memories was not about stockings all being hung by the chimney with care or dancing sugar plums swirling around in my head. It was about an incredible surprise and what I learned at a very young age.

Our family was not well off and we did not have extra money for Christmas gifts. My mom worked full-time and raised five children. She always did her best to make Christmas time special for us despite our poverty. She would sit for hours after work and knit us hats and slippers. She knit me socks to wear inside my holey winter boots to keep my feet warm. There is one particular Christmas that stands out for me. Mom and I were in the living room, I was doing homework and she was knitting. All of a sudden, we heard a loud knock at the door. It startled both of us as we rarely had company.

We both sat still for a minute looking at each other. There was another loud, 'knock-knock-knock.' I put my brave face on and headed for the door. I could be very mature if I wanted to, after all, I was 7 going on 8 years old. Mom stood up and slowly moved towards the door. We both peeked out the window and saw a police cruiser sitting in our driveway. I ran to another window to look so I could see more clearly.

There were two police officers standing at the front door. My heart started to race. Mom and I both stood quietly thinking that perhaps they would go away. The knocking got louder and louder. I was getting the impression that they really wanted us to open the door. It seemed our mysterious uniformed visitors knew we were avoiding opening the door.

Mom and I hesitantly crept our way over to the front door. She was moving very slowly. It was like a slow-motion video watching her get closer to the front door. This was very out of character for us both to be opening the door and giving them the chance to traipse in for no reason.

She deliberately opened the door just a smidgen. You could see the bright sunshine glow breaking through the crack and coming in as a stream of light. I had a feeling that the stream of light was telling us that everything would be okay.

Just as Mom opened the door, I heard an officer say, "Hello there, my name is Officer Martin. Is this the Carver Residence," he queried, even though I got the impression he knew that it was.

Mom sheepishly answered, "Yes." I could see her head nodding up and down in acknowledgment that the officer was at the right place.

Mom was likely nervous and wondering why they were there, as we would have regular visits from the Children's Aid Society. She probably thought that one of the neighbours called them to check on the well-being of my siblings and me. Sometimes we would have a representative from the Children's Aid visit us randomly with their notepad of questions. They would mention to Mom that if she did not take good care of us, we would be placed in another home. Mom worked hard and did her best but my father, whom we called "Sir", was an alcoholic with a bad temper and no patience. He had beer and cigarettes on his shopping list before milk and bread. "Sir" taught us to be very wary of police officers.

One time, I saw him get into a physical fight with 4 Police officers at the end of our driveway. They ended up taking him away in a cruiser. That occurrence is why Mom was reluctant to answer the door.

The officer who was speaking to my mom was very tall, he had dark hair and he wore a freshly pressed uniform with an added red Santa hat on his head. He had a pleasant smile. He winked at me and said, "We have a delivery from Santa. It's a little earlier than usual but Santa did not want to forget about all the good little kids in this neighbourhood."

I was in total shock. I was told by "Sir" that the police were our enemies. Now they were bringing us a gift? What was that about?

The officer handed my mom a huge basket full of fruit, nuts, cookies and cakes. It had the biggest red bow on it that I had ever seen.

He mentioned to Mom to just wait here as he had even more gifts from Santa in the trunk of his car. He and the other two officers headed down the stone driveway to retrieve another overflowing basket. This one was brimming with toys, candy, and wrapped presents. My heart raced as I danced up and down with excitement. I couldn't wait to see all the different presents Santa sent to us.

I was giggling loudly in delight. Just seeing these huge baskets of Christmas abundance made my heart happy inside. Even though the police visit to my house to offer Christmas gifts was mystifying me. I did not understand how the police received the presents from Santa this early. Or, how Santa and the police coordinated all of this?

How could bad police officers, as "Sir" told us, be so kind and full of joy? "Sir" had caused them so much grief over the years with what Mom called "his shenanigans" and now they were offering gifts at our front door to us like the three wise men. Was this some kind of trick? Maybe they had the wrong house or maybe we had to pay them back somehow? It seemed all too good to be true.

Confusing thoughts kept circling around and around in my head. Mom always seems more stressed at Christmas as I overheard her say to service companies calling and wanting payment for overdue bills. She often explained to these callers with the line, "I am not sure how we are going to make it through the holidays with no money for gifts."

Or she would say, "Keep on dreaming," when I would ask for something. When Mom would say these things to me, I would say to myself – "This is not the way my life will be when I grow up." I was certain of that. Then I would picture myself all dressed up, living in a nice modern-style home in a lovely neighbourhood. In my imagination, my cupboards were filled with all my favourite foods. I would reword her negative phrases in my head and say to myself, "No, Siree. I am going to have a Christmas tree with beautiful lights, and oodles of presents underneath for all my family and friends. My Christmas holiday will be full of surprises, joy and love. I will have plenty of food and gifts to share with anyone I choose. I will always have abundance, be able to give to others and live in a state of gratitude."

It was fun deleting Mom's negative sayings and replacing them with my happiness phrases. Sometimes I would even sing the new positive affirmations to myself when I would jump rope. I would picture the holiday as a glorious experience to be celebrated with food, music and dancing with all my family and friends.

The officer dropped off the second holiday basket at the door. I let out a larger scream of delight. I was so excited to touch and smell each item. Some items I had never seen before. I had no idea what they were. There were candy canes and chocolates, colouring books, children's games and a Barbie doll. All for FREE! I was beside myself pondering, "How this could be?"

Out of nowhere, good things do happen and they can come to us from perfect strangers who "Sir" would have us believe to be untrustworthy. These uniformed strangers made my dreams come true.

After the officer wished us a happy holiday my mom's face turned bright red. She was like a rag doll bringing the baskets into the house. The happier I was the more she told me to settle down.

I thought she would be ecstatic. I said, "Mom, isn't this great? Now you don't have to worry about Christmas this year. It is a gift from heaven."

Mom sat the baskets down on the table, lit up a cigarette and muttered some phrase about us being a charity case. Off to the bedroom she went probably embarrassed by this display of kindness. I was confused as to why she was so unhappy and not grateful for this bountiful gift for all to share.

I was thinking to myself, "Did this all come from my wishes and positive declarations that I had been rhyming off to myself before the Christmas holiday? Maybe." I waited about an hour and then went to see if my mom was any better. She was so sad. I tried to fix her gloomy attitude by making her a treat. So, I pulled a chair up to the cupboard to reach the instant coffee. She looked tired. I thought I would make her a coffee and that would wake her up. I presented her with a coffee and cookies from the gift basket. I added extra sugar to her coffee. For some reason, I thought if I added extra sugar, it might compel her to have a sweeter mood. I have no idea why I was thinking that.

So that night before going to sleep I knelt down beside my bed and prayed to whoever was listening to me. I thanked the police, the angels, and God. I even thanked the charity people not really knowing who they were.

The next day Mom lightened up a little, took most of the items, put them in her bedroom but left a few in the bottom of the basket for us to share. That afternoon, my brother and I arrived home from school early and we were so hungry. We were all alone. We looked in the cupboards and in the fridge, but there wasn't much to snack on. So, we snuck into Mom's bedroom and looked inside the closet. There were the two huge baskets filled to the brim with many treats.

We did not want to get into trouble so we didn't open any packages. We looked in the basket and found some loose walnuts. We were not really familiar with these kinds of nuts. I thought to myself there must be a way to open them. We tried hammering on one of the nuts with one of my shoes by hitting it. I tried biting it with my teeth. That didn't work. Then I tried pressing it with a book and hitting it with a screwdriver. I even tried to open it with a can opener. I kept looking at that walnut thinking, "How do squirrels open them?"

When none of these ideas worked, I asked my brother to sit in the old wooden rocking chair. He looked at me with a funny face and we both started to laugh.

I said, "I think I know a way to open these nuts."

He chuckled and gradually pulled himself up on the faded-out cushion that was hanging on the front of the rocking chair. I asked him to please sit still. We both began laughing. It was not easy to line the walnut up with the rail of the rocking chair. I would place the nut and he would rock slowly. The walnut would glide across the dusty hardwood floor and wind up under the table. It was not opening.

My brother was getting frustrated but I assured him that this would work. He just needed to keep rocking. So, he did. After about seven tries we both heard a cracking sound. A large part of the walnut went flying across the room. The other half was right in front of us. I danced with joy while I retrieved both pieces to share. Oh, what a delicious treat.

To me, it was not only about eating the nut, it was also about accomplishing something that seemed difficult. I remember really liking the feeling of confidence from experiencing the success of finally breaking it open. It made me see clearly that if you don't give up and you keep trying -- goodness will prevail.

Mom saw this as pity but I was lucky enough to see past that. I saw this as an opportunity to trust and to be grateful for the precious gifts that come our way. Following my intuition opened me up to a state of appreciation. I learned not to worry about what others think or say but instead to feel from my heart and not to judge by what I had been told or taught. I saw that the world is a kinder place than my previous experiences suggested. I opened up more and more to new experiences and new ways of seeing life. I found it exhilarating to be in a state of gratitude for those Christmas baskets and for the amazing memories of those times. I still find it exhilarating as I write these words.

I would say that the best opportunity offered to me as a child was the fact that I was not born with A BEAUTIFUL PINK WAND OF PRIVILEGE.

It turns out I was blessed with a POWERFUL ATTITUDE AND POSITIVE ENERGY - no wand required.

LIFE AFTER NEAR-DEATH
By John Jinks

In 2011, my mother had planned to spend the winter in Florida. Since she would be away from her children and grandchildren during the holidays, she chose a November date to have Christmas dinner with the family.

My younger sister was responsible for picking up our brother and bringing him to the restaurant for dinner. She repeatedly pressed the buzzer at his apartment but received no response. She tried calling his cell phone, but there was still no reply.

Worried that something had happened, she contacted the building's superintendent, who reluctantly allowed her into his apartment. Upon entering, she found him lying on the floor, speaking incoherently. Her initial disgust, thinking he was drunk, quickly turned to concern as she realized he had suffered a stroke.

That November evening went from joyful to heart-wrenching as our family shed tears, wondering if he would ever recover from this life-altering event.

For the next two months, my wife and I visited my brother almost daily as he embarked on the challenging journey of relearning how to walk and talk.

It was a long tedious process, but as time went on, things started to improve. Progress was gradual, but the results were amazing.

When he was finally released on his 50th birthday, my brother still had a slight stutter and required a cane for mobility, but otherwise, he was perfectly fine.

Life has moments when a single event profoundly impacts us. What used to irritate us suddenly feels petty, and what was once significant appears trivial.

We pause to examine our lives and reassess our priorities. As we question, answers gradually emerge. We ask and contemplate: What if the stroke had happened a day earlier? What would we have encountered that November evening? What if it had occurred a day later? What would have unfolded then?

But it didn't happen earlier or later; it occurred precisely when it did, for a reason. He received the necessary help.

Though I didn't fully grasp it at the time, I later found solace in knowing that Providence's hand was at work on that cold November night.

Albert Einstein once said, "Coincidence is God's way of remaining anonymous."

Anonymity and God do not belong together.

God rightfully deserves all the Glory for the miracle that transpired that day.

GHOSTS OF CHRISTMAS PAST
By Kim Cubitt

Christmas. Once, it possessed a special magic and nostalgia that she missed over the Holidays. Every year since that magic had been cursed, that special time of year had sent her into a tailspin instead of celebration, floating from one intense emotion to another.

It started with everyone asking, "What is the true magic of Christmas," and not realizing how that one simple inquiry could hurt. Once, Joy had been content with her reply. She used to tell everyone that it was the only question in the world with no correct answers because the magic meant something different to everyone. She had known what it meant to her once upon a time. Now, the magic had been severely diminished and there was nothing she wouldn't give to recapture it.

She missed that certain belief that Santa was magical and if she was good and made a wish, he might grant it or at least bring her something equally as loved. She ached for the family time that was shared around a special meal where everyone came together, left their phones in another room and wanted to spend time catching up on all they had missed with each other and the open kindness and well wishes between strangers.

It would be eight years without her mother this Christmas.
The loss was hard to carry for Joy as her mother had also been her best friend. The once magical time of year was now a kaleidoscope of shifting, mercurial emotions.

The first year had been a blur. The second was harder as her loss was fresh, but she was no longer numb. Year three and four she kept herself so busy she had no time to feel and that had helped her to cope. It was no more than a band-aid over her grief. Year five had been the hardest. It had felt like a milestone and it had left her reeling despite how distracted she had tried to stay.

Year six had felt hollow and somehow fake, but last year…last year something had happened, something she could only believe had been magical and for a fleeting moment, she had felt that same old elation, comfort and thrill.

It had started out so emotional. There had been a sadness inside her that she couldn't shake. The world had moved on, new traditions had been established, but she had not. Joy had adapted and made sure not to let everyone see those moments of weakness where she still cried, feeling ashamed and scared of ruining the special day for others. She had gone through the loss of three of her grandparents, three uncles and several pets over time, including one very special heart dog that had gotten her through the loss of her mother and was still that one pooch she compared all pets to that had meant the entire world to her.

Missing so many and seeing so many ghostly, empty places around the table where loved ones should still be, had made last year hard for her. The meal, though still good, was not the same. Thankfully, catching up with everyone had still made her smile and had given her heart a touch of lightness it had sorely needed.

Joy always tried to make her mother proud during the Holidays and last year had been no different. There had been gifts with forethought bought for all in the hopes they would be loved. Cookies and treats, home-baked, though she was certainly no gourmet. She had still assembled the tree in her mother's favourite spot in the window and put up the stockings, played the Christmas carols and even sang along. She put on a Santa hat and delivered gifts, set up visits with friends, sat down to catch up with everyone about what was happening in their lives and still did the big family dinner. She mailed gifts to those who no longer lived close by and set aside time for calls with them. She sat under the lights of the tree and filled out cards and wrapped gifts and stayed up well past midnight on Christmas Eve, watching old holiday movies on television.

It hit her hard that this year, there would be another empty seat at the table as her last grandparent, her mother's mother, had passed in the spring. Joy was dreading facing that new void, but thanks to last Christmas, she also dared to hope that this year, the magic would make an appearance for her again as she pulled out the wrapping paper bin, her thoughts drifting back to that morning. She had stayed up late on Christmas Eve, wrapping the last couple of gifts for her father and the fur babies, placed them under the tree, turned out the lights and had tiptoed to bed.

That night was the first time during the Holidays since she had lost her mother that she had fallen asleep without crying. Joy had made one special wish as she drifted off, the same one she asked for each year. It was the one thing that Santa could not bring her. More time.

Joy wished for one more Christmas with those she missed. Time meant more precious memories and that was what she really wanted and the one thing that could not be bought or wrapped.

Joy thought that maybe Santa had finally heard her last year. There had been a moment when she first woke up on Christmas Day, where she thought she had heard a light footstep above her. She had come upstairs and for just a moment, had smelled coffee, though none had been made as her father was still sound asleep.

She had turned to the tree on that grey morning and had flicked on the twinkling bulbs.

For just a moment as she had turned back to the room, there had been a blur, a sparkle against the wall in what had been her mother's favourite chair as if the lights from the tree had winked back at her from that spot. There was a ghostly echo of soft Christmas music in the air, although the radio had not yet been turned on and then, there had been a warmth like a hug surrounding her and the faintest scent of her mother's favourite perfume and hand cream had tickled her nose just as the sun had broken through the clouds and painted the floor of the room with golds and reds.

For just that one moment between awake and asleep, the magic of the Holidays had been restored when her mother visited her for one more Christmas.

CHRISTMAS MIRACLES HOPE FOR THE HOLIDAYS!
By Tammy Brazeau

Many of us relate Christmas to a happy occasion, time spent with family and friends. This is supposed to be one of the most special times of the year. The celebration, the gifts and the togetherness. The laughter of the children playing. The music playing, the joy and happiness on everyone's face. How beautiful. This is what most people have or want. The perfect Christmas gathering with all gifts, the huge Christmas dinner with all the fixings. The cheers. Having a wonderful time, just like we see in the movies.

Wasn't it supposed to be like this, like in the movies? What happened? Why was I always sad or concerned something would happen? Because it did. The togetherness and happiness were not always the case at Christmas for me. Fear of the unknown was how I felt at Christmas. The unexpected thought, "But what if I was worrying for nothing?" It was like clockwork almost every Christmas. The feelings of sadness, fear, and the fights, are devastating.

Most of the year, abuse survivors may be able to avoid estranged family members, but there is an expectation that they will put the past aside at Christmas. It's not always that easy. In some families, the fact that the Christmas holidays trigger trauma, highlighting family dysfunction and complicated emotions is a struggle. The powerful memories of their childhood were discouraged during the holiday season.

Seeing the lights, the sounds, the smells. These little touches around the house make it smell and sound like Christmas. The decorations, the mistletoe, the symbol of love keeping the magic alive at Christmas? Holidays bring up vulnerable feelings and emotions that lead to an increase in PTSD symptoms in some trauma survivors.

My very first Christmas with my husband. Christmas music playing, lights on low, Christmas tree lit up, wondering what is this all about. I hated Christmas. I was a bit unsure about how I felt at that moment. The feelings, the rush of emotions, tearing up, this is exactly what my beautiful mother tried to do for us. Thank goodness for her, her beautiful soul, and her instincts to always try and protect us and try to make us feel better. Making extra effort for us girls. Buying exactly what we asked Santa for, even though she probably couldn't afford it. It didn't matter to her, she wanted to make sure her girls experienced the Christmas magic the way it was supposed to be.

I remember the one year, I think I was 8 years old, I wanted a Barbie so bad, and I got one! I was so happy. I remember crying. My mother thought I was sad, but I wasn't, instead, I was crying because I knew this was a lot of money. She said it didn't matter as long as I was happy. She wanted all her girls to be happy at Christmas.

Moving forward to a Christmas with my husband, as the kids were waking up, very young at the time, 9 and 3 years old, they were slowly coming up the stairs, barely awake. You could see the excitement on their beautiful little faces. Their eyes were so big as they saw all the gifts under the tree. The joy and happiness on their faces is something I will never forget.

The day was spent happily watching them play with their new toys and enjoying each other's company. I fell in love with him all over again. This is what it was supposed to feel like. Christmas is supposed to be filled with joyful emotions.

I think about this every year. I will never forget it. The memories we made, and the time spent together was the most amazing feeling. The laughter and the feelings of wanting to be together with family was unbelievable. One of my greatest gifts was being blessed by being a stepmother. The love and joy I felt still warms my heart, even all of these years later, the kids, now grown, and having children of their own, making my husband and I grandparents. This isn't something you can describe to anyone. It's the best feeling in the world. No gifts can replace the love you have for them and they have for you. We are truly blessed.

Watching the kids open their gifts and being so thankful for everything, even socks! LOL What an amazing feeling, The love, the happiness, it's indescribable.

My mother, my sisters and I have each other, and our beautiful families. That's all a person really needs during the holidays, like Christmas. Family that's enough!

We've all had our own families to celebrate these beautiful holidays with but we get together and celebrate too. We always seem to make too much food, but we enjoy every minute of togetherness on these special days. That's the only gift we need in life. Being together with our loving family, that's it!! Nothing more nothing less. If you have been blessed to have friends like family, then you're golden!!

Family togetherness and love for each other, that is all we need.

Remember, if you know someone who suffers from abuse, trauma and terrible memories from Christmas, show them that this is not how most people feel about Christmas. This is a joyous occasion, a celebration and the gift is spending time together without bad memories.

Some of us have been through a lot. Maybe you've experienced trauma. Perhaps you, like some others I know, have not had multiple adversities in childhood experiences. Coping with trauma, and seeking support from friends and family or other people you trust can help you. Take some time alone to reflect on the experiences and try to identify what you are feeling. Life after trauma is a rollercoaster and it might take time.

Try journaling, this is a good way to manage stress and move through complex events. Face your feelings, prioritize self-care, and be patient.

Trauma is the lasting emotional response that often results from living through a distressing event. Experiencing a traumatic event can harm a person's sense of safety, sense of self and ability to regulate emotions and navigate relationships.

Lean on your loved ones for support.

A note to anyone who needs to hear this;

We don't 'get over' or 'move on' from our trauma, we are forced to make space for it. We carry it. We learn to live with it, and sometimes we thrive in spite of it!

Perhaps the butterfly is proof that you can go through a great deal of darkness yet you become something so beautiful.

Let us all remember the true meaning of Christmas,,,,

LOVE ………

that's it…………..

Christmas Miracles

CHRISTMAS ANGEL
By Mélanie Beamer

My mom will always be my Christmas Angel. She always radiated love and joy. Her passion for Christmas began all year round as she gathered the gifts throughout the year. Her devotion and passion for the festivities began in July with Christmas movies, followed by decorations and festive music in November. By December, the house was filled with the aroma of freshly baked goods.

The magic of her Christmas spirit enveloped our home. Christmas Eve holds a special place in our hearts. After the church service, we would gather around the kitchen table filled with Québec tourtières, savoury chicken pies, and an array of mouth-watering desserts. The real magic happened when we opened our gifts. My mom loved seeing the sparkles in our eyes and the excitement of gratitude. The celebrations went beyond the festivities of Christmas Day. On December 31st, we would receive our Christmas stockings, which extended the holiday spirit into the New Year. She knew how eagerly we had been waiting to receive our stockings. The stockings were filled with lots of goodies: a box of pink elephant popcorn, a box of Cracker Jack popcorn, a book of Life Saver candies and a few other treats. We also had a few new toys and a new pair of socks.

My mother's love of Christmas went beyond the decorations, the music and the gifts; it was about being there for us even during the hard times.

I remember Christmas of 1980 when the church and Salvation Army lent a helping hand. My mom poured her heart into making that Christmas special, teaching us that the true essence of the season was the unconditional love we shared as a family.

Her passion for Christmas evolved throughout the years as our families grew. She was determined to pass on her traditions to her grandchildren. When I was expecting my first child, who happened to also be the first grandchild, her passion to find something new to add to her Christmas tradition had begun. That summer, she found a beautiful snowman-shaped Jell-O mould at a yard sale. This Jell-O Snowman quickly became a beloved symbol of our holiday gatherings. Year after year, her Mr. Bonhomme de Neige Jell-O mould took centre stage, evoking smiles and laughter.

The table had other Christmas staples like her savoury and delicious deviled eggs, tasty tourtières and her famous homemade cheesecake, all lovingly prepared. Her commitment to fostering family togetherness during the holidays never wavered. Her unconditional love was the glue that held us close together.

Life had its twists and turns. In September 2022, we received the news that our dear mom had been diagnosed with Stage 4 cancer. Her prognosis was grim, giving her three months to live. My mom insisted that we celebrate her life, focusing on the joy rather than the sorrow. Despite her pain, she radiated positivity and courage. She met and held her first great-grandson. She was grateful to have many friends and close family members visit, which lifted her spirits. My mom and her loving husband decorated their Christmas tree together. She got a chance to watch some of her favourite movies. My mom transitioned to the Heavens in early December 2022.

My mom was not here in person to celebrate Christmas Eve, but she was here with us in spirit. Christmas Eve, that year, was my grandson Hayden's first Christmas. I was determined to create a new family tradition for my grandchildren. With the guidance of my Christmas Angel, I found a Heart Jello mould at a local thrift store. I knew this was a sign from the heavens, sent to me by my mom with unconditional love. I have now started a new Christmas tradition for my grandchildren. I was happy that I began my new family traditions as a grandmother.

The next miracle happened on Christmas Eve when my grandson came into the kitchen wearing a shirt that said: "Promoted to big brother." Another grandchild was on the way to join our family.

All I asked God and my mother for Christmas was for my youngest brother and his family to be at her funeral. My mother, God and another Earth Angel made this happen. My brother and family made the journey safely, even if they had arrived just after the funeral services. My Christmas miracle was extended into the New Year, celebrating and spending quality time with my brother and his family. My mother intervened from the Heavens, as she always loved to extend our holidays into the New Year. I will be forever grateful for these miracles. Merci infiniment, ma belle maman d'amour.

A few weeks before her passing, she called me with such excitement. "I have something to share with you, Mélanie. I can feel wings starting to sprout between my shoulders. I believe God has plans for me once I get to heaven. I will be an angel of unconditional love." As a Medium, I see and communicate with the spiritual realm. She has visited me many times since she crossed over and has made her appearance known.

A few months after her passing, a miracle occurred, as she woke me up in the middle of the night to share with me her transformation. She had indeed received her beautiful white and golden fluffy wings. She was an angel floating by my bedside with the biggest smile, sparkling eyes and a bright golden hallow of light surrounding her. Her mission is to send unconditional love to her loved ones and all of humanity who are open to receiving her unconditional love here on Earth. She mentioned she will be busy learning all the new skills and to remember that time does not exist for her like it does for us here on earth.

The next miracle happened on August 8th, 2023. I was reading the stories before the launch party of "Forever Changed," another collaborative book I am an author in, when my mother appeared beside me. "Mélanie, I want to let you know that the baby is on her way very soon."

On the evening of the birth, my mother woke me up with a gentle voice, so as not to wake up my grandson who was sleeping in our room. "Congratulations, grand-maman Mélanie! Gracie arrived an hour ago. Look at your phone! You have a message and a beautiful picture of your granddaughter." Then she vanished.

Miracles happen endlessly in our lives. I am grateful and blessed to have my mother as my Christmas Angel. I can call upon her at any moment.

CHRISTMAS IN THE SAND
By Sarah White

Like most people, I celebrate many traditions throughout the year. Most of them are celebrated with my family and friends. A couple of my favourite traditions that my family and I have are: cakes at birthdays, leaving cookies and milk for Santa on Christmas Eve, extended family meals at Thanksgiving and Christmas, eggs poached in maple syrup at Easter and having a movie day with my mom and my sister on the last day of summer break. Those would be considered the "Common Ones" for me. As much as I love those examples, my personal favourite tradition is the one that my parents have started with my sister and I…celebrating Christmas in the Caribbean.

For more than twelve years my parents have taken my sister and I on a holiday, either for Christmas or New Year's Eve to an all-inclusive resort in either the Dominican Republic, Cuba or Mexico. I am excited to share with you some of my favourite memories of these vacations as well as some of the life lessons that I have learned over the years and their effects on my life today.

If you have ever travelled to an all-inclusive resort, you can appreciate everything that goes into the trip. From packing a week early, to clapping while the plane lands, everything is memorable and "makes the vacation." These are memories that I hold onto and think about often. For example, I am not an early riser, but on the morning of our vacation, I will be the first to wake up at 1 a.m., ready to go with no issues because I am filled with excitement and anticipation.

I remember the very first trip that we took. I was approximately eight years old, and I saw from the window of the airplane, the most beautiful palm trees. My parents had shown me pictures of them and said that they would look different from the trees we have here at home, but to see them in person was so amazing! I am certain that everyone on that flight that day heard my squeal of excitement. Who knew there were so many kinds of trees in the world?

Life lesson number 1: If you're happy, show it and don't hide it.

I remember asking my parents many things during these trips. The most important Christmas questions I had for my parents were - Would Santa know where I am? Does he know where Cuba is? Will someone watch over our home in Niagara while we're away? - It seems so silly to me now, but it was very important for me to make sure Santa knew where I was and he knew where he would leave all of our goodies. Little did I know, Mom and Dad had it all under control. You should have seen my face when I witnessed Santa arriving at the resort by jet ski and not a sleigh led by Rudolph, lol!

Life Lesson number 2: Santa will get there whether it's by sled pulled by a red-nosed reindeer or a jet ski riding the ocean current!

I am thankful that over the course of these vacations, I learned a lot about the different cultures and how everyone can celebrate differently. On Christmas evening, I learned a valuable lesson. I had received a little Cuban Barbie doll from Santa, and I made a fuss that she was not something that I had written on my wish list. My dad pulled me aside and had to explain to me that it was not fair for me to be upset over receiving this gift. As I mentioned, I was only 8 years old and I did not understand what he was trying to tell me. He had explained to me that it is not about what the gift is, but the thought that counts. That there are many kids in the world that do not receive any gifts at all on Christmas and here I am complaining about the one I did receive. Looking back, I'm embarrassed by how I reacted but I am so grateful that my parents were able to show me how excited the other kids were to receive those dolls. I wish that everyone could teach their own children the same lesson, but if they are not exposed to it, they will never know. I know now that my parents wanted to teach my sister and I many things at a young age that we could only learn by seeing the world.

Life lesson number 3: always be thankful for what you have. You never know about other people's situations.

With every trip we took, I was getting older, I started to understand more and look forward to these trips. Not only was I excited about the 24/7 snack bar, tropical sand and the never-ending children's drink of "Miami Vice," but I was also excited about the new memories we would create as a family. A tradition that I started myself was getting my hair braided by a local resident on the beach. I thought it was the coolest thing to be able to show off to my friends at school when I returned home. On more recent trips my mom and I would get a massage together while the others would go on a boat excursion.

Our family always found one staff member at the resort that stood out to us. One that went above and beyond throughout the course of our vacation. One year it was a gardener, he would work around the clock in the heat to make sure that the resort had the most beautiful flower arrangements and that all the grass was cut. Another year, it was our maid who came to clean our room and another it was the head chef at the restaurant, who would personally bake me gluten-free pancakes knowing I had an intolerance. To thank them, we would bring them a little token of appreciation. I remember always asking to be the one to give it to them. Each and every one of their smiles are engraved in my memory to this day. We left gifts for the maids and even something for their children. For the gardeners, we would bring them a pop from our mini fridge in our rooms. They were so grateful. I know for me, a pop on a hot day is the best.

Life lesson number 4; kindness always comes back to you. You give some, you will get it back.

We made many trips to local villages during our vacations. One year, we even hired a taxi driver and he personally drove us to some places where tourists typically don't visit. We hand-delivered some clothes, candies and toys. Does anyone else remember those stuffed animals that you could also play with online called Webkinz? Yep! I was the child who had 10 of those. I stopped playing with them and so my mom thought that it would be a great idea to pack them up and I could hand them out to local families and children. As sad as I was to separate from my toys, the look on the families' faces when I got to hand deliver my stuffies to these kids was something I still think about. I know we made a difference on those days.

Lesson number 5: The smallest gesture goes a long way!

While jotting ideas down for this chapter, I reached out to my parents and asked them a couple of questions regarding the trips we took. What stood out to me the most was when I asked them why they wanted to take my sister and I on these trips. They answered by saying that they wanted us to experience new things, things that we are not typically exposed to. Thanks to them, I grew up learning about a different culture. I learned how to say some words in Spanish and I was able to see how some of the local families in these countries lived. For example, on a guided tour through a local neighbourhood, we saw a house where a family of eight lived in a house smaller than our own, with multiple family members sharing the same bed. In the words of my mom, who is also an author in this book, "I wanted these trips to include some educational lessons. I could not think of a better geography, political and history lesson to give the two of you. I wanted you to understand how fortunate you are and how other cultures can have so much less than us and they are still happy."

I experienced it all right in front of me. I got to feel and see the crystal blue ocean, I got to swim, snorkel and see the most beautiful coral reef and the fish that swim beneath us. I got to try many different foods which included real chocolate that came from the cocoa bean. I also learned very quickly that I am not a fan of big waves and catamaran boats. Best of all, I learned that giving is MUCH better than receiving. Isn't that what Christmas is all about?

I love nothing more than spending time with my family, especially on holidays. I am thankful that my parents gave me the opportunity to experience these vacations which have become a very memorable and educational part of my childhood, and I love to share them with others. The activities I experienced, the new relationships created with families and the lessons that I learned are all individual miracles that make up Christmas for me. I will forever be thankful for everything I have. Thank you, Mum and Dad, for giving me these memories. I will never forget. Although Christmas travel traditions have changed due to Covid-19, the joy I share with my family has not. We purchased a real Christmas tree in a small town where my dad would get it when he was young.

But, the biggest change of all for me has been being able to experience Christmas not only with my family but with the family of my partner. The excitement of all of the hustle and bustle and making time for both families in one day. It's a beautiful chaos that I am so lucky to be a part of and able to create new memories. I mean hey, last Christmas was spent in my apartment, snowed in and without power, due to an extreme snowstorm for three days. But a Christmas miracle came through and I was still able to see my family for Christmas dinner. As much as I miss the sand, I am happy with how my holidays are spent at home too. I can't wait to see what tradition I will start with my future family.

Happy Holidays!

TROPICAL TRADITIONS
By Emilie White

The late Jimmy Buffet once sang, "Mother, mother ocean, I have heard you call, wanted to sail upon your waters since I was three feet tall." For as long as I can remember I have always loved the water and have heard its call. Whether in a pool, in a lake at the cottage, working as a lifeguard or by the ocean, the water called me. Little did I know how much the ocean would become part of my Christmases.

In 2005, my parents took the risk of booking a trip to the Dominican Republic with my sister and me for Christmas, not knowing if we would even like it. Christmas break was one of the only times that both my sister and I were off school, and my parents had time off from work to take a family vacation. I remember them explaining later on how anxious and scared they were to take us, their two young girls both under the age of 10 (at the time) away for Christmas. Away from snow, family and the typical holiday morning. I could only imagine what they were feeling taking us on an airplane for the first time to a third-world country. I will always remember Mom handing us candy by the bag to chew during take-off and landing. I especially recall Dad telling us to flap our arms to help the plane take off. I couldn't be more grateful for them taking that leap and booking our first trip. Over 12 years of going down south for the holidays has become something I am so blessed to talk about and now write about.

The trips were something that we got to look forward to as a family, especially the few trips when my grandmother Léona, or other family friends would join. With every trip also came new firsts. The first time Sarah and I got our hair braided. The first time we learnt how to snorkel. The first time we tried new foods. Not to mention the first time we got drunk poolside. Mom always says, "It's about the experience."

We stayed at all-inclusive resorts in either the Dominican Republic or Cuba and one year we went to Mexico. We got to learn about different cultures, and we were exposed to true poverty and how the locals lived in those countries. Dad always made sure we tried different foods and Mom was on top of packing the ketchup and peanut butter because we couldn't get those down there.

The first trip was definitely a culture shock for my sister Sarah and me. We weren't sure what to expect regarding the "Dominican Santa" that Mom tried to prepare us for (I'm not even sure if Mom and Dad were prepared.) Safe to say it was not what we thought, especially since he arrived on a little boat and not on a sled with Rudolph and the other reindeer. He did in fact have a bag of toys, but Mom and Dad had to explain to two upset little girls that Dominican Santa has a more Dollarama-like workshop for toys. After some explanation of Dominican culture, Sarah and I enjoyed our trip down south. That first trip made Mom and Dad realize that we didn't need to have a Christmas tree, we didn't need the snow or even be in our home in Niagara Falls to celebrate. Sarah and I were happy on the beach, under the palm trees and creating our own traditions.

I have too many memories from these trips to mention all of them, but I will share some memories that have become part of who I am now. I have always liked pineapple, but I fell in love with the fruit while on one of our first catamaran excursions. Dad and I always shared catamaran days together, it was our favourite excursions to do while Mom and Sarah enjoyed the resort spa. On one particular trip, after snorkelling, we had some of the freshest and juiciest pineapple we have ever tasted. It might have been because of the salt on our lips or just the fact that we were really hungry, but I will never forget how amazing that pineapple was.

Also, whilst on a catamaran, I experienced what sailing felt like. On our way to our destination, the boat captains would always use the motors but on our way back we would simply sail and let the wind guide us. Nothing is more relaxing and soothing than being on the open ocean, with some strong drinks and listening to some Caribbean music. Every trip came with a different catamaran experience, but I'll leave out the time we went on the catamaran with a friend while she was hungover.

Some of the best memories came from excursions. We got to learn how to bargain when going to markets and shopping areas. One excursion brought us to the Brugal Rum Factory in Puerto Plata where we got to see how the rum was made while having a tasting. We also got to see how cigars were made in Cuba. Our taste buds really burst when we were in Mexico and had some amazing margaritas. I still have the stuffed seal I got as a souvenir when we went to Ocean World during our first trip to the Dominican Republic. I will never forget the smile on Sarah's face when she was able to figure out how to paddle board on her own.

Mom always made sure we got to see and appreciate how the locals lived. A few times we did excursions into the town and got to visit the homes of locals. Mom would bring some old clothes and Sarah and I would bring old toys to give to families we would come across. It was truly eye-opening to see how poor some people are living, but it felt good to donate some of our things to them. Mom also donated small tools and necessities to workers and housekeepers at the resorts. I'll remember the smiles of gratitude on their faces forever.

Sandy Feet Beach Bar. The name says it all. That was a restaurant Dad and I discovered while on a walk down the beach of our resort one year. A little hidden gem we fell in love with and returned with

Sarah and Mom multiple times that trip. Cold colas and cervesas were enjoyed by all.

Christmas lights in palm trees, swim-up bars, memorizing the lyrics to "Féliz Navidad," awful tan lines, cheap souvenirs, coming home after a trip and opening all our gifts at 2 a.m., and the absolute best company are all factors that made Christmases perfect. It may have looked like we were pulling a Christmas with the Kranks but I wouldn't have had it any other way.

As the years have gone by and global pandemics occur, we haven't taken a trip over Christmas in a few years. This just means that I will have to continue this tradition with my own family one day and take my parents with us. I am forever grateful and blessed to have had these trips and experiences to look back on. They truly shaped me in ways I don't know how to explain. Until next time ocean.

THE REAL CHRISTMAS

Christ came in a baby's form,
born in a stable that wasn't very warm,
placed in a manger for His bed
where people worshipping Him said;
"This is the child, Jesus,
He's the Messiah that God promised us,
Let us rejoice and celebrate
for this present so amazing and great."
Yes, this Christmas, may we gladly
remember when
Jesus was born to save all men,
Because He is the reason we celebrate
each year
for this heavenly gift of love came
down to us on earth here.

Sherry Harle

THE BLESSING OF MY LAST RAFFLE TICKET
By Sherry Harle

It was December 1977. The Red Cross Youth group that I belonged to in high school was raffling off a pretty tabletop ceramic Christmas tree that lit up. Tickets were $1 each. I was down to my last ticket to sell. What to do? Immediately, I thought of my nine-year-old cousin, Wanda. Her father had died earlier that Spring, I would buy it for her. It seemed like the right thing to do, so I did.

A few weeks later, it was the day of the draw and at 3 P.M., our principal announced over the P.A. system, "The winner of the ceramic Christmas tree is Wanda F." I was shocked and overjoyed at the same time! I couldn't believe what had just happened!

Christmas finally rolled around and our family visited Wanda's family. While there, I looked around and my eye fell on a familiar sight that was on the window ledge, twinkling brightly. It was the ceramic tree! I felt so good.

Many years later, I still marvel at God's creativity in moving my heart to buy my last raffle ticket for a little girl to help put a smile on her grieving heart to show how much He cared.

What a great God I follow!

DON'S CHRISTMAS
By Linda Rodgers

The story of my Uncle Don's Christmas miracle began on July 4th, 2013. Don was in surgery. A Whipple procedure was being performed to treat pancreatic cancer. Doctors hoped the cancer hadn't spread beyond the pancreas, but the 12-hour surgery was cut short when they discovered the disease had spread and was beyond treatment.

Don woke when the fog of anesthesia gradually wore off. He assumed that the mere 4 hours spent under the surgeon's knife represented good news. However, while he was in recovery, the doctor had spoken to his wife, Barb, who had been burdened with the gut-wrenching truth.

Unfortunately, the reason for the abbreviated surgery was far from good. Both were devastated by the grim prognosis that meant Don had only 5 short months left to live, a timeline that now hung heavily over both their hearts.

Never had they imagined Don would be the first to go. Throughout their long marriage, he had taken care of Barb who battled the relentless grip of COPD and was not expected to live into old age. This shocking plot twist was very cruel indeed. As they processed the tragic news, a heartfelt request came from Don. It was a simple plea, but one filled with so much heartache.

"When the moment arrives" Don quietly implored, "I want you to tell me when it's time to let go."

This pledge would become a sacred promise that Barb would fulfill on the fateful night when Don drew his final breath.

Before that sombre event, Don made the most of his remaining days to reconnect with friends, family, and with God. Even though Don hadn't stepped foot in church since the passing of his mother, he nonetheless felt the urge to make peace with his past. Therefore, he booked an appointment to meet with the leader of the church. Sadly, Don was not alone in his suffering, nor was he alone when he visited the priest that day. In truth, he was accompanied by another man who shared his pain and had also come in search of solace within the walls of the church.

Don was the last child to be born into a family of 9 children. He was a surprise baby who arrived after his older siblings were having children of their own. Consequently, Don's nieces and nephews were nearly the same age as him. When Don visited the church that day, it was his nephew Denis who had accompanied him. Tragically, Denis was also dying of cancer, which touched Father Julian profoundly. Because of their shared grief and suffering, Denis and Don referred to themselves as cancer buddies.

When I asked my Aunt Barb about her husband's journey, she affirmed that he had never felt sorry for himself. Her eyes glossed over as she expressed her admiration for this man who lived each day to the fullest. She loved his sense of humour most of all and spoke with tearful pride of his ability to maintain his sarcastic wit despite the illness. Barb added that he accepted and embraced his fate and even helped to plan his own funeral, making the whole process as pleasant as possible for those he loved.

Evidence of Don's devotion to his family was obvious long before the illness. He was a talented musician who played several instruments and performed in many bands during his adult life.

However, he happily gave it all up when he almost missed the birth of his grandson Bryden. This child was the centre of his world, and Don couldn't bear the thought of missing a single moment of his time with him. Don's profound love for his grandson saw him through many difficult moments, but even that great love was not enough to spare him from his fate.

The diagnosis changed Don's entire outlook on life. He made the most of his last days to have meaningful conversations with everyone, including his cherished daughters Laura and Katelyn.

The bits of wisdom Don shared were parting gifts for his loved ones. No words were left unsaid, and he made sure that all who visited also had a photo taken with him. He freely shared his love and asked for nothing in return but was blessed with an unusual gift from a special visitor, nonetheless.

Don received an astonishing revelation during one of his many visits. A niece had come from out of state and was accompanied by a psychic medium who made a startling observation. The woman asserted that Don's late mother was by his side. Moreover, his mother had a comforting message to share with him. She wanted Don to know that she was waiting for him on the other side and that when he was ready, he needed only to raise his arms and she would be there to welcome him home. This detail would prove important later as Don approached his end of life.

With each passing day, Don became weaker and the pain became more unbearable. The tumour was making it difficult to eat and Don's body wasted away. Then, in yet another painful twist of fate, Barb experienced a health crisis of her own that landed her in the intensive care unit, struggling to survive. But Barb would not be without her beloved. Within days she defied doctor's orders and left the hospital to be at her husband's side. Barb returned to find her husband standing in the kitchen. Somehow, he had found the strength to prepare a meal to welcome her home. He was making pasta sauce, a family favourite, and a Sunday ritual he was determined to execute one last time.

Don's end of days were spent in his family home, surrounded by loved ones and in the care of exceptional nurses who later admitted that Don was their favourite patient. How could they not love this big teddy bear of a man who still had so much zest for life? Don knew that time was not on his side, and this painful truth was made clear in early November when his cancer buddy Denis finally succumbed to his illness.

Even though Don was declining rapidly and approaching his own final days, he wouldn't be deterred from attending Denis' funeral. Denis was loved by many, and the line of persons who came to pay their respects extended out into the parking lot. As Don approached the open casket, he was overcome with grief. He reached in to hug his departed nephew and sobbed uncontrollably. "I am so sorry buddy," he said, "I'll see you soon." There was not a dry eye in the room, and sadly, this was the last time my Uncle Don left his home.

Don was not expected to survive another Christmas, so the family decided to celebrate it a month sooner. Regrettably, Don knew even that date would be unattainable therefore, Don's Christmas took place on November 18th, 2013. He didn't ask for much but insisted there would be plenty of food for the guests even if he couldn't enjoy a single bite himself. Christmas music played softly in the background as guests attempted to invoke a festive feeling. Denis' widow was also in attendance and was doing her best to celebrate the day despite her recent loss. There was even a surprise visit from Don's niece and her two girls who had come carolling to brighten the celebration.

Within days of that early Christmas, the pain had become too much, and Don was placed in a medically induced coma. But before he was rendered unconscious, the family was called to his bedside.

Don had a few final words to convey, and he expressed his love and gratitude to all. Don asked my father to take care of his girls after he was gone. And his last words to Laura were, "Have a nice life kiddo."

Don languished in a vegetative state for another week and on the night of his passing, he was once again surrounded by close friends and family as one by one, each bid him farewell. Barb was true to her word. When the moment arrived, she asked everyone to patiently wait outside so she could speak privately with her husband one last time. She held his hand and gently whispered "It's time for you to go." It wasn't long after, that all in attendance witnessed the unbelievable. After being in an induced coma for an entire week, incredibly Don tried to sit up.

He also tried to raise his hand and even smiled a little. A short time later, he was gone. His mother had come to take him home.

Don's Christmas became a new family tradition. To this day, the family still gathers on November 18th to share food and memories of this beloved man. But the real miracle actually took place 5 years later.

Katelyn had married and was expecting her first child. It was a girl, and her name would be Charlotte, Charlie for short. Her arrival was expected in mid-December, but the pregnancy had been incredibly difficult for both mother and child. Katelyn had endured two carpal tunnel surgeries, Bell's Palsy, and dangerously high blood pressure. In addition, the gestational hypertension caused intrauterine growth restriction which halted baby Charlie's development.

Doctors wanted to induce labour early, but Charlie was still too small and too fragile, so they held off another week. Eventually, the risk for mother and child was too great to postpone the delivery any longer. Therefore, induced labour commenced on November 28th, but it didn't take.

A second attempt to kickstart Katelyn's labour took place the next day, but it seemed that baby Charlie was planning to have a different birthdate. The challenging pregnancy culminated in a life-threatening emergency. Katelyn's placenta had ruptured, and the umbilical cord was wrapped three times around the infant's neck.
Unbelievably, Charlie was spared from any harm, but the same could not be said for her mother. Katelyn had begun to hemorrhage and lost nearly one and a half litres of blood. Over the next hour, she clung to life as the medical team worked furiously to save her. Katelyn was in and out of consciousness until the next day, but would eventually pull through. It was a miracle they both survived.

Charlotte Noelle was born on November 30th, 2018, exactly 5 years after the passing of her grandfather Donald Noël. Their survival was an early Christmas miracle. One that none of us doubt was orchestrated by Don himself. Though Charlie's grandfather had passed long before her debut into this world, you would never know this based on the relationship she continues to have with him. She talks to his photograph, as though he had been there all along, and nobody questions the love she holds in her heart for her beloved Papa Donald.

In loving memory of my aunt Barb (Jun 1961- Sep 2023) who left us before I could share this story with her, to finally reunite with the love of her life.

THE BIRTH OF JESUS FORETOLD
By Bill Harle

God sent the angel Gabriel to Nazareth,
a village in Galilee
to a virgin whose name was Mary.
She was engaged to a man, Joseph
was his name.
From the house of King David, he came.
The angel appeared to her and had
this to say,
"Greetings favoured woman, great are
the LORD's blessings that have
come your way!"
Mary was greatly troubled by his words
and wondered about this kind of
greeting she had heard.
Gabriel said to Mary,
"To be afraid, I don't want you to be
for favour with God, you have won.
You will conceive and give birth, Jesus
you will call Him, He is God's Son.
He will be great and as the Son of the
Highest He'll be known
and the LORD God will give Him His
Father David's throne.
And Israel He will reign over,
His Kingdom will never end but go on
forever!"

Then Mary said this to the angel
wanting to understand,
"How can I have a baby for I know not
a man?"
The angel did reply,
"The Holy Spirit will come upon you and
you will be overshadowed by the
power of the Most High.
For this reason, the child shall be holy.
Called the Son of God, He will be.
Remember your relative Elizabeth who is very
old, she who has no children.
She has conceived a son and this is now
the sixth month for her, she
who was called barren.
What is found here we see
is that with God nothing impossible will be."
Then this response came from Mary,
" I am the LORD's servant, may your word
be fulfilled in me."
And then after these words she did impart
the angel from her did depart.

(Lk 1:26-38) rhymed

THE BIRTH OF JESUS THE MESSIAH
By Bill Harle

This is how the birth of Jesus the Messiah, came to be.
His mother Mary was engaged to Joseph but before
they were married, by the Holy Spirit,
made pregnant, was she.
Joseph her fiancé was a just man
and he did not want to disgrace Mary publicly
so to break the engagement privately,
he did plan.
While he was thinking about what this may mean
God's angel spoke to him in a dream.
He said, "Joseph son of David don't hesitate to wed Mary
for it is by the Holy Spirit this Child was conceived by,
that she does carry.
Mary will have a Son and to Him the name of Jesus
you are to give
because He will save His people from their sins
so eternally they'll live."
All this happened to fulfill what the LORD through
the Prophet Isaiah had to tell:
"The virgin will give birth to a Son and they will call
Him Immanuel.
(The meaning of this name is this –
with us, God is)"

When Joseph woke up, he did what the angel
of the LORD did command.
He took Mary home to be his wife and him to be
her husband.
Not until she gave birth to a Son, they as one became.
And then Joseph gave to Jesus His name.

(Matt 1:18-25) rhymed

THE BIRTH OF JESUS
By Bill Harle

About that time the Roman emperor, Augustus
ordered that throughout the Roman Empire
there would be a census.
To register in his own ancestral home
everyone had to be.
So, Joseph had to travel to Bethlehem, David's
hometown, going there from Nazareth
in Galilee.
Joseph was a descendant in David's line.
He went with Mary, his fiancée, who was
pregnant at this time.
While there, to give birth, her time came.
She gave birth to her firstborn son and
Jesus, they called His name.
In strips of cloth, they snugly wrapped Him in.
They laid Him in a manger because there was
no room for them in the village inn.

(Lk 2:1-7) rhymed

JESUS'S BIRTH
By Bill Harle

The angel assured them, "Don't be afraid
for good news of great joy, I bring
to everyone!" he did say.
"In the city of David, a Saviour, Who
is Christ the LORD, He is born
to you today.
And to you, this will be a sign:
wrapped in swaddling cloths, lying in a
manger, a Babe you will find!"

(Lk 2:10-12) rhymed

Christmas Miracles   Page 133

THAT FIRST CHRISTMAS
By Rose Bourassa

It's always difficult when you lose a loved one. The pain remains whether the loss is expected or a sudden surprise. Adjusting to a new life after loss is always difficult, especially that first year.

Year one is challenging. Adjusting to life without someone makes getting through the holidays even more difficult, especially when that death happens during the holiday season.

My son died the week before Thanksgiving. His funeral was on the Tuesday of Thanksgiving week. We tossed our plans for the traditional family Thanksgiving turkey dinner with all the fixings and dined on leftovers from the reception. There was nothing happy about that Thanksgiving. Even with a place at the table reserved for him, someone decided they needed to sit in that spot. That empty place setting meant nothing to anyone other than us.

We managed to get through Thanksgiving and then proceeded to focus on Christmas. My heart and soul were not into decorating the house or a tree. Weeks before the accident, I volunteered to decorate a tree for a community event. That tree was to be auctioned off to help raise money for needy families. I'm not sure how it happened, but with the help of my florist friend, we decorated the tree beautifully. Had it not been for her, it certainly would not have been as lovely as it turned out.

Having done that, my resolve to celebrate Christmas further waned. I had a daughter and granddaughter who needed to celebrate Christmas. All my brothers and sisters, the nieces and nephews, and the grandnieces and nephews always celebrated Christmas Eve at our home. I had no desire to deal with all those people in my home. Their being there meant that I had to decorate and put up a tree, shop for gifts, wrap them, and cook a meal, including desserts. What was I to do?

The Christmas Tree auction was ten days before Christmas, so I bid on the tree we had decorated. Not only had I donated all the decorations for the tree, but now I was paying for everything again to avoid decorating another tree. It was a lovely tree, though.

Instead of shopping for gifts, all the children under 18 received a gift card for Christmas. It was so much easier for me when I had no desire to shop and wrap. For the adults, I arranged a white elephant gift exchange. You needed a simple, little generic item that would be placed in a pile for adults to pick from. It was nothing fancy, with a low dollar amount per gift. And it was not mandatory to participate either. If you chose to join in the fun, you brought an exchange item.

After all the children had opened their gifts, we moved their mess out of the way for the adults to take over. All the white elephant gifts were piled on the living floor for everyone to study. We had gift bags full of tissue paper, small and large boxes, some with bows, some without. Somebody beautifully wrapped a package in gold paper with a stunning gold bow. Indeed, that would be amongst the first items chosen.

All the adults pulled a number from a bowl. The rules of the exchange were simple. You picked your gift and unwrapped it for the group when your number came up. The person with the following number had the option to select a new package or steal one from someone who had already opened one. Any gift stolen was subject to two steals before it became the property of the owner of the second steal.

With over a dozen gifts to select from, the simple hot chocolate set was the item everyone seemed to want. Through all this, the gold package was untouched. I was last to pick. So I took the gold box. It was heavy. The bow easily slid off. My curiosity was piqued. What could this weighty box hold? As I slowly unwrapped the package, I saw that it was suited specifically to a male.

My daughter was intently watching me from across the room. She saw what the item was and what the package contained at the same time I did. As tears began to fall, she said, "Don't cry, Momma." Try as I might, the tears escaped. The entire room now focused on me and the package in my hands.

This non-generic package contained a gift set of "Axe" men's products—aftershave, cologne, and soap. For a guy, this was certainly a great gift., but not for me. However, I was very familiar with the scent. There were times when I loved it and others when it made me sick. But every time I smelled it, it was always worn by the same person, my son.

As challenging as that first holiday season was, he had somehow instructed someone to purchase this set and arranged it so I would be the one to receive it. It turned out that my nephew, who was also my son's godfather, was the purchaser of the gift. He has no idea why he felt compelled to purchase it, but he knew he had to. Little did he know that was his godson's favourite scent.

This was a sign from him to say that, although someone had sat in his chair at the dinner table, he would not miss Christmas with the family. He knew a little hello from heaven was needed to soften the pain I felt during this Christmas season.

HOPE IS A CANDLE
By Susan Diane

The season of advent has a special luminance as I wait for the birth of my first child.

Joulupukki, the Finnish rendering of Santa Claus, may bring the baby early, it may be my Christmas miracle. Or perhaps my child will be the first newborn of the new year. I would be glad of that; we could make good use of the generous gift basket received by this celebrated arrival. If I must stop working, Taavetti's income is enough for necessities, and even a little extra, but it will be easier with the money from my employment at the boarding house. I will carry my baby with me in a portable cradle my husband has fashioned for this purpose, so I can go about my daily routine of cleaning and serving up meals. I plan to work with almost no pause providing there are no complications.

The midwife assures me our firstborn will be a healthy boy. There is no certainty, but it is good to hear her reassuring words. It makes my beloved smile, sweetly and softly, the wonder that this child will be, after so many years on his own. When we married, he was already thirty-four years old, and after his recent birthday, he is thirty-five. He was accustomed to his life as a solitary bachelor and now expresses without reservation and repeatedly the marvel and pleasure of the companionship of his young wife heavy with child. Until recently, and for the fourteen years since his arrival in Copper Cliff, he worked hard and unceasingly, returning weary each evening to his sparse room in this spartan establishment. It was clean and the food was sustaining but only simplicity and necessity were evident. The addition of a wife is a long-awaited and desired revision to his routine.

Whatever I conjecture about the future, soon I will hold my precious child. Already I love him without reservation. I have made knitted booties and bonnets and sewn cotton shirts and little leggings in abundance and our few friends have brought gifts of clothing and handmade toys. He is a much-anticipated new member of our small community. We are a family, and the family is growing. I sit quietly and I am crying. I hold the surprising store-bought teddy bear that was delivered today by my sister-in-law. My tears fall on his tiny honey-brown body.

With a red and white striped scarf, he is dressed up for Christmas. I name him Nalle, the Finnish word for teddy bear and I cuddle him on the top of my belly alongside his future playmate.

Reluctantly, I place him in the carved wooden cradle, welcoming widespread limbs waiting.

Without warning or reason, I feel an unanticipated flicker of joy brighten my heart and a spontaneous sparkle of amusement flashes across my serious and sensible, often seemingly sombre, countenance. It ends at the upturned corners of an unbidden sudden smile. I am an enigma of ever-shifting emotion. Other, older women assure me this is to be expected in my condition.

It is our first Christmas as a married couple. Serene and solemn, we move out of the church sanctuary into a white winter wonderland of new fallen snow. Under the carpet of sparkling crystals, there are patches of smooth and slippery ice. I am so close to my delivery; it would not serve me to fall. I am supported by the strong arms of my husband, and we walk cautiously. As we make our way carefully home, I am softly singing my favourite carol, "Jouluyö, Juhlayö". Taavetti insists I settle myself on the small sofa in our sitting room, once my tiny bedroom. With the baby imminent we have reclaimed my former bedroom, and I have accepted a reduction in my wages for the extravagance of occupying two rooms. He brings our traditional Christmas Eve banquet on a metal tray festively adorned by a white crochet cloth: pickled herring, small round boiled potatoes, turnip casserole, carrot salad, hot fresh rye bread, rice porridge and warm mulled wine. Always thoughtful and generous my doting husband presents me with a beautiful lambs' wool shawl. It is soft to the touch, sea blue and white weave with a decorative fringe, the colours of the new Finnish flag. Resting against his solid shoulder I read aloud the letter I received from my mother earlier this week, full of news and maternal advice. I saved this letter for after the busy bustle of Christmas preparations, now I can savour this too infrequent pleasure. With two wonderful gifts and my first baby soon to arrive, I am truly fortunate.

It is the first Saturday of January.

"The midwife assures me I am not due to deliver our son for another two weeks." My own calculations suggest that my baby is due to arrive this weekend, but I keep this idea to myself.

"You are very large my wife. I think it would be good to spend a quiet evening at home." His brow creases with worry as he regards me from across the supper table.
"But the movie is showing only this weekend, and who knows when I may be able to go out again." Even to my own ears, I sound whiny.

"I know how much you love the story of the lost boy and his tiny fairy, but it is cold and icy, and shouldn't you be resting?"

"It will be a welcome distraction. After this waiting is done, there are many nights ahead when I will have to remain home." I do not want to quarrel. It is unlike me to insist against my husband's good counsel.

His eyes soften and I see his resolve is weakening, I speak again. "It is only for a few hours, and we will be sitting most of the time."

"It is a worry to me, but I won't refuse you this small thing. Maybe it is better for you to have some diversion."

We are comfortably settled in the cinema. I lean to rest my head on Taavetti's chest, and he lays his arm protectively about my shoulders. The film has begun. Looking up I speak so only he can hear me.

"We don't even need to read the captions; we know this story well." At times even the silent films are a challenge to follow, with our still limited English.

Tinker Bell is dying from the poison intended for Peter.

I read the words on the screen aloud. "If you believe clap your hands …" I begin to clap my hands and nudge my husband to do the same.

"Don't let Tinker Bell die." I continue to read aloud. Along with many others, I am now clapping vigorously, and no one objects to my speaking aloud.

"If we clap, she will get well again." Taavetti smiles indulgently at my side, but he does not join with me and other members of the audience who respond to her plight.

"See her light is growing stronger." My face grows hot and flushed. Our collective effort is rewarded, and the petite pixie flickers brightly as she accompanies Peter to rescue Wendy and the boys.

"So much can be accomplished if we only believe." My cheeks are moist with happy tears.

My eyes are bright with tears as we board the tram. "It is so sad that Peter returned alone to Never Never Land."

"Foolishness." His tone is gruff but the twinkle in his eyes assures me he finds this folly endearing. "You have a tender heart; you will be a kind mother."

"When our son is born, it is a tale I will tell him as I rock him to rest."

We ride in silence and soon we are stepping off the tram in Copper Cliff. We walk hand in hand in the crisp cold night, it is only a few blocks to home. When we turn the corner to our street I stop suddenly and hold my hands to my ample belly.

"Ooh!" My countenance contorts with pain as I feel my first contraction.

In a few short hours, as the sun rises on the first Sunday of 1925, I greet my son. The story of his birth is an interesting part of our family history.

Author's Note: This story is a work of historical fiction. Any resemblance to actual events or persons is a coincidence.

THE CHRISTMAS THAT WOULDN'T HAVE BEEN
By Iantha Jinks

So why help the less fortunate at Christmas, we all know it's coming people should be prepared right! Well maybe you have had those thoughts too but you can make a difference in someone's life and you may not know the ripple effects that may have.

You see many years ago, what seems like a lifetime ago, I was struggling. I was a single Mom who always ran out of money before the end of the month. I couldn't manage to pay all the bills and keep food on the table for my kids and forget about any extra activities. Even paying the $2 a week for scouts was a stretch.

Then things went from bad to worse, I got sick, I couldn't work, and I didn't even want to go out of my house most of the time, especially not to a grocery store. I would have panic attacks just being worried that I didn't have enough money to pay for the food. As Christmas drew nearer, the panic attacks got worse, there was no way I was going to have enough money to buy gifts when I couldn't even afford food. Of course going shopping was out of the question. I needed a Christmas miracle like I had never needed one before.

Just a few days before Christmas my phone rang, and I actually answered it. Often times I wouldn't because it might be a bill collector. However this time it was a delivery service asking if I would be home as they had a delivery to drop off. This was years before Amazon would deliver every day. I wondered who was sending me something. It wasn't long and the delivery man was ringing my doorbell. He brought in not one, but 3 boxes. In these boxes, there was all the fixings for a wonderful Christmas dinner and enough food to last us about a month. There were also wrapped gifts with my children's names on them, not just one each but multiple gifts each. As well, there were fruits, candles and little items to go into their Christmas stockings. The card read "Because we know you needed it this year" and no names. I later came to find out that a group of my co-workers had made this happen but wanted to remain anonymous.

So now, many years later, I am sharing this story to let you know that you too can make a difference in someone's life. Ever since that year, I have always tried to pick up some extra gifts to pay it forward. For over 10 years, we have been doing this by donating to our Church's Christmas Eve dinner for those in need in our community. Everyone who attends gets a full Christmas dinner, a gift and a bag full of goods, such as socks, hats, mittens, toiletries, candles...

Last year marked the 30th year that the Niagara Worship Centre has been hosting this event. What started as just providing for a few people who were alone at Christmas has grown to over 500 people the year before COVID-19, and although the number has dropped, there are still hundreds that attend, then leave fed and with a bag full of goodies. If you know of someone in need or if you would like to donate please reach out to NiagaraWorship.ca or call or drop off at 6846 Frederica St, Niagara Falls, ON.

If not our Christmas giveaway then please find one in your community and make a donation, you can make a difference one gift at a time, one life at a time.

MISTER POSTMAN STOP AND SEE

By Iantha Jinks

Let me introduce you to my friends, Dianne and Brian Harrison. Each year, this couple is instrumental in arranging a team of people who write thousands of Christmas and Holiday cards for our Canadian Military who are stationed abroad at Christmas.

This all started one Christmas when their friend whose son was stationed overseas asked his mother to send cards to the others in his division who had no one to send them a card. The following year after their friend passed away the Harrisons picked up the baton and have continued by heading up this labour of love for almost two decades now.

This summer this wonderful couple was awarded the Queen's Jubilee Award for this as well as all the other amazing ways they volunteer and help others in their community and around the world.

You may not be able to go abroad to serve your country but you too can encourage and support those who do.

Diane and Brian Harrison

UNEXPLAINED GIFT
By Jody Swannell

"Vicky: Do not open until Christmas!"

The label on the package was typed in a common font with no return address. Vicky turned the package over trying to determine where it came from and who could have sent it. A private courier had dropped it off, the fellow shrugged his shoulders and walked away when Vicky asked who'd sent it.

She placed the neatly wrapped, one-foot square box on her dining room table. Perhaps her husband Kyle sent it. Vicky doubted it, Kyle wasn't usually one for secrets or surprises.

Vicky's daughter Sam poked her head into the room. "What's that, Mom?"

"I don't know," Vicky said.

Sam read the label and wiggled her eyebrows at Vicky conspiratorially. "Let's open it."

"Christmas is tomorrow—I'm sure we can wait that long." Vicky rolled her eyes.

"Maybe it's from Dad?" Sam suggested.

"I don't believe so."

Vicky stared at the plain beige paper box, puzzled. I'll open it tomorrow. She thought to herself. If whoever sent the package knew her, they knew that she wasn't very patient. She supposed that the only reason it arrived on Christmas Eve was that all delivery services would be closed on Christmas Day.

***

Just before midnight Vicky, Kyle, and Sam sat at the kitchen table watching the time.

Sam fidgeted impatiently in her chair. "Come on twelve o'clock… I'm dying to see what's in there." She set her elbows on the table and put her chin in her hands.

Kyle picked up the box and inspected it one more time. "It sure is light for its size."

Earlier the family had decided they would all stay up and open it just after twelve so they could sleep knowing the mystery was revealed, without spoiling the intentions of whoever sent it. When the clock officially ticked past December 24th, Vicky unceremoniously ripped open the package and removed a mini cranking mechanism that appeared to belong to a music box.

Sam stood up and held out her hand "Let me see, Mom. What is it?"
Vicky handed the instrument to her daughter and searched the paper stuffing once more for clues as to the purpose and origin of this strange gift.

Kyle scratched his head thoughtfully. "Strangely unconventional."

Sam turned the tiny crank arm and the tune Für Elise by Beethoven started to play. The high-pitched music sprinkled throughout the kitchen, and immediately Vicky felt an unexpected rush of joy. Sam on the other hand didn't seem too impressed.

"Lame," Sam said somewhat disdainfully. She kissed Vicky and her dad, scooped up the cat, and trotted off to bed.

Vicky looked at Kyle. "How odd—I know this song. What I can't figure out for the life of me is why in the world someone would send this to me."

Kyle picked up the little metal gadget and inspected it closely. "Does the music mean anything at all to you?"

"No not that I can think of. It's one of the many pieces of music our class studied years ago in high school. It's familiar, but I can't recall any special significance."

Vicky put the device in the china cabinet while Kyle recycled the cardboard. They went to bed wondering who might have sent it and why. Neither of them could solve the puzzle so they shut off the lights and went to sleep.

***

The next morning Vicky sat up so abruptly that it caused Kyle to jump out of bed confused looking around.

"What's the matter, what happened?" he asked.

Vicky stared blankly at her husband for a moment before she clapped her hands together and laughed jovially.

Kyle misunderstood his wife's behaviour and turned to check himself in the mirror. "What are you laughing at? My hair is slightly messy but not enough to warrant that reaction."

Vicky grinned from ear to ear. "No honey, it isn't you. I'm pretty sure I've solved the mystery box… I can't believe it! I suspect we are going to have a guest for dinner."

"Don't keep me in suspense, who sent it to you?"

"It was Aiden—I'm convinced of it. I dreamt of him." Vicky got out of bed and began to dress.

"Who's Aiden?" Kyle raised an eyebrow.

Vicky ran her fingers through her hair. "A boy from an African village that our high school class donated to years ago. We organized a fundraiser and wrote letters to the children living there. Each of us received a letter in response, thanking us. My letter was from Aiden."

"Really? So, what makes you think the music box was from him?" Kyle asked.

"In my letter, I wrote about how I struggled with the Beethoven sheet music I was working on. I'd completely forgotten about it." Vicky smiled.

"I see, it was the same piece of music. Okay, I'll bite… it's been many years since high school, how could he have found your address?"

Vicky sat on the edge of her bed. "I'm not sure. He wrote a sweet letter to me saying that, thanks to our class, he would be able to go to school and that he planned to become a doctor. He promised that he would travel to Canada to meet me once that happened. This was just before the Christmas holidays, and I had sent my letter in a Christmas card with a snowy scene. I imagined that he'd never seen snow before."

"You think he's coming here, after all these years?"

"I'm certain of it. He appeared in my dream--it must be him." Vicky grinned with confidence.

The doorbell rang and Kyle's eyes widened. "No way," he said in disbelief.

"I've got it," Sam called out.

Vicky rushed down the stairs to catch up with her daughter just as she opened the front door.
"Hi, can I help you?" Sam asked not recognizing the man before her.

Aiden stood smiling proudly in the doorway, as Vicky approached.

"Sam, this is my old friend—Doctor Aiden Nnadi," Vicky said with great pleasure.

WE HAVE INCLUDED SOME PAGES FOR COLOURING AND ARTISTIC EXPRESSION.

PLEASE ENJOY THEM!

Christmas Miracles

Christmas Miracles

Page 162

Christmas Miracles

Page 163

Christmas Miracles

Page 164

Christmas Miracles Page 166

Christmas Miracles

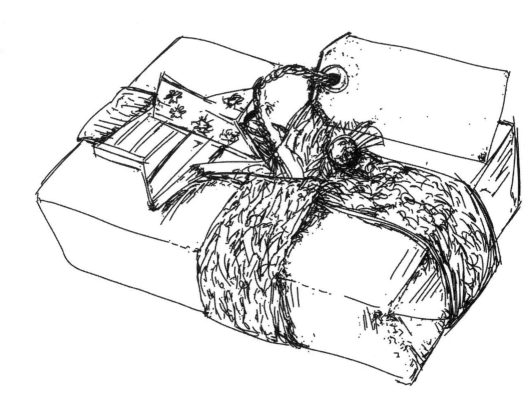

Christmas Miracles　　　　　　　　　　　　　　　　　　　　Page 171

Christmas Miracles

Page 172

Christmas Miracles

Page 176

Manufactured by Amazon.ca
Bolton, ON